ONCE UPON A
SURE THING

LAUREN BLAKELY

ALSO BY LAUREN BLAKELY

Big Rock Series

Big Rock

Mister O

Well Hung

Full Package

Joy Ride

Hard Wood

One Love Series dual-POV Standalones

The Sexy One

The Only One

The Hot One

Standalones

The Knocked Up Plan

Most Valuable Playboy

Stud Finder

The V Card

The Start of Us

Every Second With You

The Seductive Nights Series

First Night (Julia and Clay, prequel novella)

Night After Night (Julia and Clay, book one)

After This Night (Julia and Clay, book two)

One More Night (Julia and Clay, book three)

A Wildly Seductive Night (Julia and Clay novella, book 3.5)

The Joy Delivered Duet

Nights With Him (A standalone novel about Michelle and Jack)

Forbidden Nights (A standalone novel about Nate and Casey)

The Sinful Nights Series

Sweet Sinful Nights

Sinful Desire

Sinful Longing

Sinful Love

The Fighting Fire Series

Burn For Me (Smith and Jamie)

Melt for Him (Megan and Becker)

Consumed By You (Travis and Cara)

The Jewel Series

A two-book sexy contemporary romance series

The Sapphire Affair

The Sapphire Heist

ABOUT

It's so easy being best friends with a gorgeous, talented, charming guy.

Said no woman ever. Except me.

My friendship with Miller is a sure thing — he's my plus one, my emergency contact, and my shoulder to lean on. He's also been by my side helping me raise one helluva awesome kid who's the center of my world.

Nothing will change our easy breezy friendship. Until I have the bright idea to convince him to start a new band with me.

Trouble is, our sizzling chemistry in the recording

studio is getting harder to ignore, no matter how risky it might be.

***

Sing sexy songs with the woman you've been lusting after? Get up close and personal as you croon to the woman you've wanted for years?

Piece of cake.
    NOT.

Performing with the sweet, sassy and insanely wonderful Ally is like one gigantic obstacle course of challenges for my libido. And my libido is one sexy love song away from kissing her senseless and taking her home.

But, I'm not a serious kind of guy, and she's not a one-night-stand kind of woman. If we cross the horizontal line, we might risk our sure thing and end up out of tune forever...

CHAPTER 1

Miller

This is the big moment.

I'm focused like a hawk on the finish line, the black-and-white checkered flag in my crosshairs. I'm ready to own it.

But the prize won't come without a fight. Our fiercest competitors steer their dingy into the stern of my boat, trying to take Jackson and me down in the middle of Conservatory Water in Central Park.

That won't do.

That won't do at all.

A surge of adrenaline rushes through me. Jamming on the controller, I gun the engine on the speedboat, powering ahead.

One length.

Two lengths.

Almost there.

Bam.

"Take that," I mutter as I jet away from the wily ones in the nick of time, gliding under the flag mere seconds before those ferocious twelve-year-olds can catch the twenty-nine-inch radio-controlled speedboat that just bested all others.

I high-five my teammate, Jackson, triumphantly. Victory tastes so damn good. "We did it! I knew we could pull it off."

He beams. "You're the man, Miller. You are one hundred percent the man."

Minutes later, the race organizers hang a medal around my neck, and I whisper a grateful thank you before they give Jackson his medal too.

This medal is a thing of beauty, and I love it. Because I love games and fun and enjoying every single second of, well, everything.

Rubbing my thumb over the gold, a rush of emotion blasts through me, that wild sensation like I'm a bottle of soda about to do the Diet Coke and Mentos dance.

There's only one other feeling that comes close to *this*.

I haven't had that feeling in years, and probably never will again, so I do my best to shove it aside.

I grab our boat, and Jackson and I head out through the park, the cool autumn breeze rustling the trees.

"What's next? Do we graduate to the Hudson River?"

I laugh. "I was thinking the Atlantic. We can race RC boats through an ocean, right? Now that'd be a helluva thrill."

Jackson claps me on the back. "It's almost the same as playing in front of thousands in a stadium."

"Oh yeah. Exactly the same," I say, deadpan.

But then, my chest starts to ache, immediately and insistently. That's odd. Because it feels like a pang.

Like I'm *missing* something.

I *like* racing boats with Jackson.

I dig that we won this competition. Yet, there's something I love more.

Something that gives me an even greater high.

That's what I miss.

I sigh heavily.

"You okay, Miller?"

I quirk up my lips, considering the question. "Ever listen to Depeche Mode?"

He arches an eyebrow. "Aren't they like fifty years old?"

I scoff. "Please. Their heyday was in the 1980s."

"You've been alive that long?" he asks as we cross over an iron bridge.

"I was alive and well in the 1980s, thank you very much."

Jackson scratches his smooth, seventeen-year-old jaw. He hasn't started shaving yet, lucky bastard.

"It's hard for me to picture the 1980s, since it was another century. Also, it's weird you were born in another century. You must feel so ancient."

I tuck the boat tighter under my arm. "I'm a fossil. I'll be eligible for carbon dating in a few more months. Anyway, I find myself listening to Depeche Mode and The Smiths when I'm not entirely content with something in my life."

"Dude, that's deep. Is this when you drop me as my big brother?" he asks, in a worried voice.

I shoot him a look like he's crazy. We've been paired up in the Big Brother program for ten years. "You're family, man. I've been keeping you out of trouble for a decade."

He laughs. "It was your influence, was it?"

I laugh too. Jackson never needed much help to stay out of trouble. He just needed a person, since his dad is out of the picture and his mom works two jobs. "Of course it was my amazing influence."

"Also, if you dropped me, I'd have to start acting out. Put the napkins on the wrong side of the plate and whatnot. Answer a question in class without raising my hand."

I shudder. "I can't even handle that kind of rogue behavior. But no, something else is making me tune into those bands. Don't get me wrong—I'm a happy camper. But I'd be happier if I had one other thing in my life." I take a deep breath, girding to spill out what I just realized. "Maybe Campbell was right."

Jackson stops in his tracks. "Whoa." He digs into his pocket. "I need to record this for posterity." Jackson grabs his phone and holds it up, ready to shoot a video. "Say it again. Admit your brother was right. I'll use this for the video component of my media scholarship application."

I wave him off. "No way. Can you imagine the hard time Campbell would give me about that?"

Jackson laughs, but persists. "C'mon. It'll be fun. It's a rare moment, you have to admit."

I shrug, and he shoots a short clip. "Fine, Campbell was right."

"Talk to me. What is Campbell right about?"

As he stuffs the phone into his pocket, I wave my free hand to indicate the lake. "I thought all these games like Monopoly and radio-controlled boats would eventually fill this gigantic hole in my heart left behind when the Heartbreakers split." I tap my sternum for emphasis. "And I do enjoy them. They are ridiculously fun, but at the end of the day, I still want something else." I can't believe I'm about to say this, but my older brother knows me well. He knows what my soul needs—to make music again. Since that won't happen with the Heartbreakers, the band my brothers and I played in for years, I have to choose Plan B. "I need to start a new band. Campbell has been encouraging me."

Jackson whistles in appreciation then gets in my face. "I've been telling you that for years, man." He pokes my chest. He pokes it again. "Years."

"Maybe I wasn't ready to hear it till now," I suggest as we head along the curvy path. "I guess I kept hoping Campbell would see the light and want to start up again with Miles and me. But he's content as a teacher and with the band he moonlights with, and Miles is busy with his solo tour. So, I need to form a new band. Something local. Something manageable. Like Campbell does with the Righteous Surfboards."

"I'm down with this. So what's the problem?"

"Here's the thing. Campbell had an idea that I can't get out of my head."

He taps his chest. "Lay it on me."

"Chances are I'll be seen as a Heartbreaker," I say, taking a beat. "*Unless* I do something different. Radically different."

"Shave your eyebrows and mime the songs?"

"No, smart aleck." I pause for dramatic effect,

sweeping my hand out wide, like I'm lighting up a marquee. "Picture this: Miller Hart and Female Singer To Be Determined. It's time for me to sing with a woman." I shoot him a curious glance, since I'm honestly not sure how someone—anyone—will react to this plan. "What do you think of that idea?"

"I'm a seventeen-year-old straight guy. Natch, I think singing with a *lovely lady* sounds awesome."

"Speaking of lovely ladies, I need to go meet Ally. I told her I'd help her with a project."

Jackson furrows his brow. "Um, to point out the obvious, why don't you sing with her? She was the Queen of YouTube."

I laugh. "Have you ever heard the two of us sing together?"

"Um. No. Has anyone?"

"My point exactly. It isn't pretty."

On that note, I say goodbye to Jackson. After I stop by my apartment to drop off the boat, I head downtown to meet my best friend.

It's a damn shame we can't harmonize for crackers.

But then again, singing with your best friend seems like a surefire way to torpedo a relationship. I've been there, done that, and have a truckload of medals to prove it.

If there's one woman I want to keep in my life, it's Ally.

CHAPTER 2

Ally

Time to bring it home. Make them feel everything.

I raise my chin, move close to the mic, and say the final words. "A fresh new hurt surged inside her from this knowledge, but with it came a bold determination to find who had ripped this hole in the fabric of her world. She would track down whoever it was, man or woman, beast or machine. And she would exact revenge. For her people. For humanity."

Dramatic pause.

"And most of all, *for him*." A beat of silence.

And I'm done.

I shove off my headphones and breathe the

deepest sigh of relief, now that I've finally, after all those grueling vocal miles, crossed the finish line.

I open the door of my booth, step into the control room, and pronounce "THEEEEEE ENNNNNND" to the gal on the other side of the glass. "That's five hundred pages of epic battles, sword fights, brutal deaths, and stolen kisses in the can."

"And that's a big old hallelujah to us." Kristy joins me in a raise-the-roof dance from her post at the sound desk.

The latest young adult fantasy novel I narrated required a full week in the booth to knock out the story of a seventeen-year-old orphan who rises above her station to become a warrior princess and save her people from intruders from another land.

At least, she does that until the cyborgs invade.

"When the publisher said it was an epic story, they weren't kidding," Kristy says, shoving a hand through her dyed blue hair.

"I am exhausted on behalf of Malindia." That's the heroine from the tale we just finished.

Kristy stares sharply at me. "There is no time for exhaustion. Tomorrow, you must return to the salt mine and play a jaded teen who inherits her grandma's doll shop," she says, referring to the contemporary teen novel that's on the next day's docket.

"Caffeine and I will be here, with bells on. Ready for the next book."

"All right, go take a break. Have some honey and hot tea tonight to treat those golden vocal cords. We need them in tip-top shape."

Kristy is my primary engineer for the young adult audiobooks I narrate. From the epic fantasies, to the space operas, to the contemporary John Green and Stephanie Perkins–style novels, she handles all of it for me, and I love her mama bear routine.

"See you tomorrow," I say as I sling my purse onto my shoulder and leave the booth, heading down the hall of the recording studio that I own an itty-bitty stake in—a stake I'd like to be larger.

Someday. I'll get there someday.

A few feet ahead of me, a young man and woman laugh then duck into studio B. They're the Cooper siblings, and I gave the twenty-something brother and sister musical duo a tour of the studio a few weeks ago when they were searching for a place to record. They were recently discovered online by an agent who now has nabbed them for several commercials, as well as a couple of songs.

They said I could pop in anytime, so I slip into the control room, whisper a hello to the engineer, and watch the pair. They look fantastic together, with a blue-eyed, fresh-faced style that matches their crystal-clear sound. My heart aches as I watch them, a pang of longing rocketing through me, sharp and sad.

Well, maybe not as sad as I'd be if I had failed at my first attempt to save the entire world from beast or machine.

But sad enough.

I miss what that duo has. I miss singing with my brother.

But life goes on, even though Kirby's moving away. So must I go on. Right now, that means trekking to the hobby shop, since I have to help Chloe build a godforsaken castle.

I tear my gaze away from the duo, head down the hall, and wave goodbye to the receptionist at Platinum Sky Studios. As I exit the building, I send a text to my good friend Miller, telling him I'm ready and raring to go. He's been expecting me.

Ally: This is the moment you've been waiting for all week. The chance to show off your prowess. Be there in thirty minutes or else.

Miller: I can leap tall buildings in a single bound, I can win gold medals in boat racing, and I can make it to the hobby shop in Chelsea in less than thirty minutes.

Ally: You beat ALL the fifth graders??? Every single one of them? I am so unbelievably proud of you.

Miller: Sixth graders too, and seventh. So there. And you thought I couldn't hold off those pesky kids.

Ally: Not true. You know I always believed in you.

Miller: You especially believe in my ability to save you from school projects.

Ally: That's scaling a tall building in a single bound for sure, my friend.

As I duck into the subway entrance, looping my brown hair, with its one lavender streak, into a ponytail, I wonder, not for the first time, what genius decided that craft projects are the gateway to understanding everything from cellular structure to history... *in the sixth grade.*

Why do kids need to craft a mailbox to look like a cat, a dog, or an actual blue postal box in which to receive Valentine cards from their classmates? Likewise, why do they need to bake a cake to demonstrate mitochondria?

It's a mystery of the universe right up there with why conditioner can never keep pace with shampoo, and why are cooked tomatoes ever a thing?

After I reach my stop, I walk several blocks in the chilly late-November afternoon, enjoying the nip in the air as I do my best not to stress about the fact that my brother is moving several states away, and that means we won't be making new YouTube videos that helped me pay for Chloe's school bill.

I'm not starving. I'm not struggling. Yet, I'm also not the one percent, and it can be hard as hell to live in New York City. But this is the life we have—the one I've carved out for her since she became mine so unexpectedly when she was only six years old.

I shove all those worries aside when I see my favorite smile.

Miller's.

It's not a lopsided grin or a wicked smirk like the heroes in the books I narrate, since apparently wicked smirks began way back in high school.

Miller's is a toothpaste-commercial smile. There is only happiness in his grin. Only delight, since that's Miller's middle name and his mantra. I've never known someone to be such a joy-monger, but that's precisely what my best friend is.

He leans against the doorway of GigiAnn's Hobby Shop on Eighth Avenue. When I reach him, that magnetic smile has extended to his hazel eyes, the flecks in them sparkling. For a moment, it's as if all my worries are gone. The man is a happiness drug.

He wraps his arms around me, warm and strong, and I hug him back, sighing contentedly.

"Congrats on your boat racing gold medal."

"It was nothing. Tell me—did you vanquish many dwarves today?"

I laugh as I unwrap myself from him. "Silly kitten, that was last week." I thrust my arm up as if I'm leading troops into battle. "Today, I took on an entire brigade of cyborgs."

He shudders. "I can't think of anyone more qualified to do that than you."

I flick my hair off my shoulder and raise my chin proudly. "I'm so adept at navigating the dangers of imagined worlds from my trusty studio C."

"How many books is it for you now? Five hundred?"

I swat his elbow. Because I like swatting him. I like nudging him too. I'm not sure why, but I do.

"Ha. You know it's not that many. I'm at one hundred forty-two books and counting. And I still haven't been hired to narrate a romance, despite submitting tons of auditions and putting the word out to all my publisher contacts."

He sighs sympathetically, knowing my dream to expand into romance has been blocked by cyborg-infested walls hundreds of feet high. "Look on the bright side. The publishers love your sweet style. You can't help it if you have the perfect voice for a teenager. It's like sugar. It's like honey. It's like a Pixy Stix, and those are damn good." He flashes that winning grin again, one that seems to say *don't worry, be happy*. "Note to self: pick up Pixy Stix for dessert."

"You have such an overactive sweet tooth."

"It's well-exercised."

"And, yes, I'm thirty-one going on sixteen vocally," I say with a what-can-you-do shrug. I've been trying to crack the romance genre for five years to no avail. I'm told my voice reads too young, too innocent for that genre. I've been working on vocal exercises to bring a tiny bit of a smoky, sexy vibe that might help me snag some romance deals. I love the work I do, and the number of great young adult stories has flourished in recent years. But I have to think of the future. What if the young adult genre goes bust at some point? What if my voice becomes overused in teen stories? I want to diversify, and romance seems the most natural segue, especially since I like romance.

Miller holds open the hobby shop door for me. "After you, my warrior princess. I believe we have a castle to create."

"Chloe left me a list of items to pick up, since she's seeing her therapist."

"Never miss a shrink visit, I say." Miller stops in front of a remote-controlled helicopter display. "How are they going for her, anyway?"

"Good. She's almost done with the appointments. She's doing so well now, but it took a while," I say, smiling as we go inside, proud of my girl.

"I'm glad she's doing better. It's all because of you."

I wave off the compliment as we head down the aisles. Pom-poms and fabrics abound, nestled alongside scrapbook boxes and glitter glue, which cuddles with glitter guns and ribbons. I stop at an aisle bursting with silver ribbons, polka-dot ribbons, and ribbons with tassels. I scratch my head. "I don't understand why there are so many ribbons."

Miller leans in close and whispers, "The better to tie you up with, my pretty."

A tingle spreads over my shoulders, surprising me, even though I'm not surprised by his words. He's a natural-born flirt, and I'm used to his naughty banter. It's never directed toward me, per se. He's just having fun. It's Miller being Miller, like when we play Bananagrams and he tries to make as many naughty-sounding words as possible, like caulk and diphthong. "In that case, let's make it a polka-dot ribbon. I can wear it with my famous polo shirts and ponytails," I say, referring to the super-sweet style I wore when I sang online with my brother.

"Ooh, that makes it even naughtier, and it proves my point."

"What's that?"

He holds up a finger. "I have a hunch craft stores are frequented by the Fifty Shades crowd."

I laugh. "DIY BDSM-ers?"

He wiggles his eyebrows. "Ribbons are for tying pretty wrists." He circles his hand around my wrist, sending another unexpected charge through me. I do my best to ignore the sensation. He lets go quickly and leads me to an aisle of wooden frames, bird-houses, and, oddly enough, paddles. "Those paddles are not for school projects, I tell you."

"Whatever are they for?" I ask, feigning innocence.

Miller mimes spanking my butt. Next, he gestures to the candle-making section. "Exhibit B that hobby shops are fronts for kinky sex clubs—just imagine all this wax dripping on bellies and butts tonight."

"How on earth am I supposed to work on a project with Chloe now that you've put these thoughts in my head?"

He runs a hand lightly over my hair and says in his raspy baritone, "I suspect those thoughts were already there."

Were they? Are they? Images scroll through my mind, mostly involving ribbons.

Miller rubs his hands together and switches gears. "Now, let's find some Styrofoam to make ramparts."

He walks ahead of me, and for a brief moment,

or maybe longer, I linger on the feel of him near me, his hand on my hair, the comment about the notions in my head. Are the notions in my head involving him?

I'm not sure what to make of this new zip that rushes through me. So I dismiss it, since that's easier. I join him in the Styrofoam aisle, where he plucks the items Chloe needs from the shelf and drops them in a red shopping basket.

I enlisted Miller's help for Chloe's sixth-grade project on medieval times, since he's absolutely amazing at building things. I suspect that's on account of the fact that he still has a ten-year-old boy inside him.

He also used to be a Lego master, and he won several Lego contests growing up. A few years ago, he showed me pictures of his creations, and I promptly enlisted him as my secret weapon in the school project battle.

As we head to the checkout line, Miller sneaks a peek at his watch.

"Do you need to go?"

He scoffs. "Please. I'm in this for the long haul, warrior princess. I'm just checking to see how many minutes until my feeding time."

Miller's stomach keeps me busy—I've learned a few tricks. "Can I tempt you with Thai or Chinese takeout tonight?"

Miller's eyes light up. "Actually, can you get that pumpkin curry dish from Avatar's Burritos?"

"Anything you want. You know the rules. I feed you, and you help Chloe with the tenth circle of hell."

"It's a fair deal to me."

As we leave and walk to the therapist's office on Sixth Avenue, Miller clears his throat. "So . . . I made a decision."

The earnestness in his voice surprises me. He sounds vulnerable. I meet his gaze and ask softly, "What is it?"

His hazel eyes look into mine. "You know how Campbell's been pushing me again to start a new duo?"

I nod, remembering that Campbell mentioned it when we met up with him recently.

Miller shrugs happily. "I'm ready. I posted an audition notice on my way down here. I'm looking for someone to sing with me, do some local gigs, maybe record a few videos, see how it goes. Nothing too crazy yet, but we can start here in New York."

I bump my shoulder to his. "Good, because if you were on the road all the time, I'd be a sad panda." I frown dramatically, but I'm more relieved than I let on that he'll mostly be around.

"You know I'd miss you, and Campbell and Samantha, and Jackson, and, hell, I'd even miss my doorman because that dude has the best advice on fantasy basketball picks."

I roll my eyes. "Glad I rank up there with your insider fantasy league coach, Miller."

He drapes an arm around me and squeezes. "Just messing with you. I'd miss you like crazy." He lets go of my shoulder. "And I decided to take another piece of his advice."

"What's that?"

He holds his arms out wide. "I want to sing with a woman."

On Sixth Avenue, at four in the afternoon, my blood freezes.

I've no idea why this news turns me to an icicle, so I do my best to find some morsel of warmth inside me. I try to muster a laugh, but all that comes out is a tight, "That's going to be great."

"You think so?"

I nod robotically. "Of course."

"Too bad we'd be absolutely terrible singing together. Otherwise, I'd say it should be you and me."

"We're like orange juice on cereal."

We've attempted karaoke. We've sung a few times at Christmas parties. You'd think we'd sound great together—he's a former teen idol who played in arenas with his brothers, and I used to sing duets to the tune of millions of views on YouTube.

But our styles simply don't mesh.

My voice is a church voice. His is a rocker's.

"You'll find someone who sounds amazing with you," I say in my best supportive tone, even though there's a part of me that desperately wishes it were me.

I wish, too, that I understood why I want that.

CHAPTER 3

Ally

Chloe emerges from the therapist's office, giving me a quick wave then shoving her sleek auburn hair off her face.

"Hey, Monkey," I say, using the nickname I bestowed on her years ago when she scurried to the top of the rock climbing wall at the park in the blink of an eye.

"Hi, Aunt Ally. Hi, Miller."

He offers a fist for knocking, and she knocks back.

"Are you ready to become a medieval architect and build the most awesome castle in the world?" he asks.

"I think so. Especially since Dr. Jane said I'm fixed now."

I laugh lightly and give her a squeeze. "You were never broken, Monkey."

She shrugs as we walk down the avenue, heading to our apartment. "I kind of was, Aunt Ally."

"No, you kind of weren't."

She stares sharply at me over her green glasses—she picked out the color to match her eyes. "Maybe a little broken? Like a plate with a crack?"

I wish I could take credit for her dry sense of humor, but she arrived on my doorstep that way. Deadpan, direct, and honest. She tells it like it is.

"Not like a plate at all," I insist. I don't want her to think there's anything wrong with her simply because life handed her a short stick when she lost her mom at age six, on top of not having a dad in the picture.

"Dr. Jane says I'm almost done, especially since I sat with Hannah and Hailey at lunch this week."

Miller cheers for her. "That's awesome. You've wanted to do that the last few weeks."

Chloe nods. "Dr. Jane said sometimes when you figure out what you want, you just need to go for it."

Once we're back at my apartment, the two of them work on the castle as I demonstrate my dinner-ordering prowess, including tracking down Pixy Stix for Miller. As they finish the castle, I grab my knitting bag and complete a pair of purple mittens I've been working on, since mittens rule. Once the project is done and Chloe is reading in her room, Miller and I play a sudden-death game of Bananagrams. We're neck and neck the whole time, but I keep thinking about the therapist's advice.

It's simple advice so I ask myself *what I want*.

I want to support Chloe, to provide for her in a way her parents couldn't. I want to make sure we always have a cushion since that's something she never had either. With my brother moving out of state, we won't be able to make our music videos, and we'll lose some of our YouTube money.

But there are other things I want too.

To expand. To push myself. To challenge myself.

Figure out what you want and go for it.

Over the next several days, as I slip into the persona of a jaded teen dealing with an inheritance of dolls, I find the answer.

There *is* something I want, and I think I know what I need to do to get it.

CHAPTER 4

Miller

I strut down Madison Avenue, listening to some kick-ass rock songs that fire me up. There's nothing like a little mix of The Rolling Stones, Foster the People, and Muse to make a day even better. I'm an omnivore when it comes to genres—rock, jazz, pop, country. If it's good, I'll gobble it up. I'm like Owen Wilson in *Starsky and Hutch*—I'll take anything.

Right now, I'm enjoying Muse's cover of Frankie Valli's "Can't Take My Eyes Off You."

As I turn the corner, the chorus blasts in my ears, I'm bouncing in my Vans, and the December sun is shining brightly. The sun knows what it's talking about because this day is going to be killer. I have a little silver laptop in my messenger bag, and more than two hundred auditions to listen to.

Life is good.

I turn into Dr. Insomnia's Tea and Coffee Emporium, where Campbell has promised to meet me later this afternoon, after I sift through the first batch of these sure-to-blow-me-away auditions.

"Hey, Tommy, what's shaking?" I say to the guy who owns the shop.

"Not much, Miller. Want the usual?" he asks, offering a hand for one of those frat-style, made-up, secret shakes. I never rushed a frat in college. I glance down at my jeans, band T-shirt, and skater jacket. I am so not a frat boy. But I know Tommy well, so I've mastered the fist-bump, slap, smack back.

"The usual sounds fantastic. Extra whipped cream, please?"

"Consider it done."

A minute later, he slides a hot chocolate to me, made with whole milk, because life is too short to waste on coffee when there is sugar. I try to pay him, but he says my money's no good here. Naturally, that makes me stuff a twenty in his tip jar. "Love you, bro."

"Same to you."

I grab a table in the back, pop on my big-ass headphones that make me look like the dude from Cloud City in *Empire Strikes Back*, and flip open my laptop. I have ladies about to croon into my eardrums, and chocolate to satisfy my sweet tooth.

* * *

Two hours later, I'm absolutely dying. I'm literally dead on the table. I am a motherfucking doornail.

When Campbell strides into the shop, I barely lift my head. He raises one eyebrow and gives me his WTH look before heading to order a cup of joe.

Nothing comes between my bro and his joe.

With the cup in hand, he joins me, grabbing a chair and swiveling it around. He pats me on the shoulder. "Do I need to call in the medics to revive you? Have you overdosed on sugar? Is this like that time when we were ten and you decided to test every flavor of Skittles?"

I snap my gaze up, correcting him. "That was important scientific research. I verified that every flavor does indeed taste different, even if I had to eat five hundred Skittles to prove my hypothesis."

"It was hilarious watching you bounce off the walls on a sugar high, but when the sugar crash hit, you tanked on the floor of the kitchen. We had to walk around your body like it was a corpse."

"Thanks for taking care of my remains so thoughtfully," I snort.

"A sugar corpse." He leans back in his chair and takes a slug of his coffee. "What's the story? Wait, don't tell. I bet you discovered the pure pain of listening to auditions?"

I sigh heavily. "I made it through seventy-two, and then I turned dead."

"You have to kiss a lot of frogs, as they say." Campbell nods to my computer. "But what did you think you'd find? An embarrassment of riches?"

My eyes widen. "Yes! I made it very clear in the casting breakdown that I wanted somebody with a voice that would rock my socks off."

Campbell bends to look underneath the table. "It appears your socks are still on. Are those squirrels on them?"

"Don't judge. They're my favorite socks. And at the rate this is going, they'll stay on me forever. How hard can it be to find a decent singer?"

He scratches his jaw. "Talent is hard to come by. I gave you a few names though."

"I know you mentioned Rebecca Crimson. She's fantastic, but she's not available. She was just signed, and she's working on her own album."

Campbell points to the computer. "By my math, you have more than one hundred left." He rolls up his shirtsleeves, brushes his palms against each other, and plugs in his earbuds so we can both listen. "There has to be a diamond in this rough."

A couple of hours and several cups of coffee and hot chocolate later, we've whittled the samples down to about eight decent auditions. Am I ever glad that Campbell joined me today. I doubt I would've had the mental fortitude to soldier through the rest of them alone.

But then again, that's sort of how things have always been.

Campbell is my rock, my partner, my brother in every damn sense of the word. That's no disrespect to Miles, who's three years younger than I am. I love that guy like crazy too, but it was Campbell and me who started the Heartbreakers, and he was always the heart and soul of the band. He sang a little more than I did and wrote a few more songs, tipping the balance in his favor. But the thing is, he never held that against me. He carried the ship, and I fucking loved him for it. He made my dreams come true.

I do understand why he had to quit, though it broke my heart. But I'd have been a total douche if I'd said that to him, or anyone, at the time. Twelve years ago, when his daughter was only two, his wife died, leaving him a single dad. He decided to focus entirely on his kid. I get that. Wise choice, in retrospect, since Samantha is one of the coolest teens I've ever known.

Campbell peers at the screen, cocking his head. "Wait. Did you see this last one?"

"Which one?"

He points to the browser. "Looks like it just landed in your inbox."

I sigh heavily. "I'm sure it's crap. We're fine with the ones we have."

He shakes his head, tsking me. "Let's listen to . . ." He stares at the screen, peering at the name next to the track. "Honey Lavender."

We both put earphones in, and with a name like that, I wait for some kind of hipster, ukulele-playing Zooey Deschanel–wannabe voice.

But that's not what happens.

When I hear the first words of a pretty love song about yearning, I zoom in on the voice, a spark igniting in my chest. Her voice sounds familiar, but different too, and I can't place it. So I just enjoy it.

It's pure and pretty, but like a good wine, it has afternotes. I can taste it, a little husky, a little smoky. It's like a sweet angel drank a glass of whiskey and laughed as she purred in my ear.

As she slides into the chorus about being tangled up all night long, I'm moving my shoulders, getting into the groove.

Campbell is too, tapping out a rhythm on the wooden table.

I point to the screen, mouthing to my brother, "This shit is good. She's the best for sure."

When the song ends, we're both grinning.

"She's like a supper club singer. You need to get her to submit a video. And the others too, just to be sure," he says.

I gesture to Campbell like he's a genius because he fucking is. "See? What would I do without you? You know exactly what to do . . . with everything. And you found this Jessica Rabbit gem."

He rolls his eyes. "You'd have found it too. You just had to get through all the others first."

"But that's what you're so good at. Well, including singing."

"So are you."

I bat my eyes. "Does that mean you 'Love Me Like Crazy'?" I ask, naming one of our greatest hits.

Campbell smiles. "Would you believe I heard that in a coffee shop the other day? I started humming a few lines while I was waiting for my drink."

I wiggle my eyebrows and sing in a low voice, gliding into the tune. "*Even though you're gone, I still love you like crazy.*"

As if he's helpless against the power of the song, he chimes in, "*All I want is to find you again, even if that's crazy.*"

I drum my palms on the table a little louder. "*Tell me, tell me, I haven't lost you.*"

He points at me, nodding in time to the music we're making. "*Tell me I'm not crazy.*"

Then we're both singing, crooning the chorus that made us millions. "*Tell me you love me like crazy.*

Tell me you want me like crazy. Because, girl, you make me crazy."

It's like we're flying downhill, the wind at our backs, the sun beating down.

This is magic.

This is my true love.

I finish with a powerful flurry of my fingers across the air keyboard, and he slashes the chords on his unseen guitar.

Applause and cheers startle me, and I jerk my gaze around. Holy shit.

We just performed an unexpected set at a coffee shop for Tommy and a twenty-something blonde in a maroon knit cap. She's standing a few feet away, holding her phone and beaming a full-wattage grin. "That was amazing. I love you guys so much. I hope you don't mind that I recorded it. It's just for me. I want to watch it over and over."

"We like to do impromptu private shows now and then for our biggest fans," Campbell quips.

Her hand flies to her heart. I do believe Campbell has just made her day.

"Thank you again. So much." She heads to a chair in the corner with her beverage.

"Sing 'Hit the Road.'"

I turn to the counter where Tommy is goading us on, smirking from behind his big beard.

Campbell waves him off. "One tune is enough for a Friday afternoon."

"Come in tonight and play a whole set, then," he says, needling Campbell more.

I'd be game. I'd happily dive into that number with him, or any of our songs for that matter. I loved nothing more than playing with him, and later with Miles when he joined us. My heart winces with longing to have that again. That's honestly what I miss most about performing. The companionship with my brothers. The camaraderie. I'm a social creature. I want to have a good time, make some music, and play with family.

But family isn't an option. Even so, I'd like to find that kind of musical *and* business chemistry with another musician. Someone who's invested, who wants to work hard at making music. Maybe I can have that same sort of we're-a-team vibe with a new singer.

Campbell clamps a hand on my shoulder, smiling. "That was fun singing together."

"It's always fun," I say, a little wistful, wishing coffee-shop improv was a regular item on our schedules.

"Truer words." Campbell hitches his thumb toward the door. "And now I need to hit the road. I'm heading to a violin lesson with Kyle, then dinner with Samantha and Mackenzie."

"Try not to have such a perfect life, will ya?"

"What can I say? I'm a happy clam." He taps the computer. "Get moving on the next phase. You want to make sure they have stage presence. You need videos, especially from Honey Lavender. Damn, with a voice like that, I wonder if she looks like Jessica Rabbit."

"Let's hope so." I shake my head. "Wait, I didn't say that."

He points at me. "You be good this time."

As a former rocker, I had my fair share of women wanting to score, thanks to my mic and keyboard, and honestly, my teen idol face. I didn't sleep around when I was sixteen. That would have been gross. But we still played when we were in college, and man, those were some fine years.

The years that came after were too, and the rock star mystique never hurt.

Trouble was, I once got involved with a drummer I played with when I went solo for a few years. She was a session musician, Tiffany Turner, and she was fiery on the drums. Fiery in bed. Fiery out of bed.

And fiery as fuck when we broke up. She stomped over to my apartment and tossed my laptop out the window. She tossed my TV and my Xbox too, sending them all crashing to an electronic graveyard of her making on East Tenth Street and Fifth

Avenue. All because I said, "I like you, but I don't want to get serious."

Eventually, I found a new drummer. But I learned a valuable lesson. Don't mix business with pleasure.

That means it doesn't matter if Honey Lavender is sexy or not. What matters most is whether she can sing well with me.

Screw asking for a video audition.

I'm ready to meet all of the top nine, because why waste time with a video when the kind of magic I'm looking for, the kind I just experienced with Campbell, is best discovered in person?

I write to the top picks, and then to Honey, asking if she can come in to do a song with me in person.

CHAPTER 5

Ally

Breathe.

Just breathe. Air comes in, air goes out.

But as I take a break from the world of night magic and rogue teen witches battling armies of spirit clones to check my email, I seem to have forgotten the basic mechanics of respiration—because of this email.

I close my eyes, will my jackrabbiting pulse to settle, and finally take a breath. I open my eyes and reread the email from my best friend. The subject line is *Blown away*.

Thought your song was fantastic! Can you meet me on Monday at ten forty-five to sing?

Then there's an address for a studio Miller likes to use.

Mine.

He must have booked the time with one of my colleagues.

I fan my face and try to collect my thoughts as excitement zigzags through me.

He thought I was amazing. He thought I was great.

I'm so screwed.

There's no way I can pull this off.

How am I going to walk into *my* studio, say *surprise*, and then knock out a song with my best guy friend as my newly created, sexier, smokier alter ego?

I mean, *obviously,* I knew this was a possibility. I'd *hoped* for this possibility.

I wanted him to pick me because he loves my voice, and if he's calling me in, it means my vocal gymnastics worked.

The key is to keep blowing him away as Honey, and Honey has some naughty in her. She has a dose of sultry, a dash of cinnamon, and a whole lot of spice.

I can't walk in there looking like Ally Zimmerman, the a cappella queen. I need to jettison the whole look and character I mastered when I was half of the family-centric brother-and-sister duo. No ponytails, no collared polo shirts, and no bouncy Keds shoes.

I won't be the soprano princess with a voice like a bell, the kind of woman who lights YouTube on fire singing "Amazing Grace" mashed up with "The Four Seasons." Or "Only Fools Fall in Love" mingled with "Hallelujah." The Zimmerman duo has nothing in common vocally with Miller's pop-rock style of big anthems and powerful songs designed to be played in arenas.

But I *can* do that stuff.

I simply need to look the part.

I reach into my purse to freshen up my lip gloss, my fingers rubbing against the stack of bills I need to pay.

Chloe's school bill.

Chloe's therapist.

Not to mention the rent.

Maybe if I sang with Miller, I wouldn't have to worry about hustling so hard for every book, every contract, and every deal.

Later, I finish fending off today's tribe of spirit invaders, and I head home. As Chloe and I plan our outfits for the Christmas party at Campbell's house tomorrow, I start to formulate my plans.

I call my friend Macy and tell her I need a little night magic.

* * *

I grew up in New Paltz, New York, the youngest of three kids to a literature professor and a dentist. My parents were and still are regular churchgoers, and that's how my brother and I started singing. Sundays, Easter, Christmas . . . those were my favorites—since our church was more casual, we sang "I'll be Home for Christmas" right along with "Oh Come All Ye Faithful."

I parlayed that love of singing into chorus in high school then an all-girls a cappella group in college.

Our sister, Lindsay, laughed at her lack of musical talent and pursued a college degree in environmental science, nabbing a great job in her field shortly after graduation. At just twenty-three, she became pregnant after a one-night stand who told her he never wanted to be a father. Determined to do it all, Lindsay managed to raise her kid on her own and juggle a career for the first six years of Chloe's life.

Until she drove to a friend's house one snowy evening in March, lost control of the car on a patch of ice, and lost her life when a truck rammed into her.

The seatbelts in the back seat did their job. Somehow, miraculously, Chloe only broke an arm.

I say *only*, but she lost so much more.

My parents are older and retired, and they offered to raise her. Trouble was, their health was on the decline. Besides, Lindsay had asked me one Christmas, as we were setting gifts under the tree, the blue and white lights twinkling in her living room.

"Will you take care of my girl if anything happens to me?"

I stared at her as if she'd sprouted a unicorn horn. "Nothing is going to happen to you. You're healthy and safe."

"You never know." Lindsay grabbed my arm, held it tightly, forcing me to look into her brown eyes. They were sad but determined. "Will you raise her? Make sure she's happy and healthy and knows right from wrong? Make sure she has fun and does all her homework too? I want you to be her guardian if something happens to me."

"Are you sick?" I'd asked, fear thick in my voice.

"No. Just trying to be smart. You never know what a day has in store for you."

"Of course. But stop talking such nonsense on Christmas."

Three months later, fate had the worst in store. Lindsay died on impact, and Chloe became mine.

Kirby and his wife, Macy, have helped over the years, taking care of her often, pitching in with bills. My parents spend many weekends with her. But at the end of the day, my house is her home. I'm the one who signs her permission slips, who's listed as the emergency contact, and who's her guardian.

Without a roadmap, I've done my best to give her stability and love. It hasn't always been easy, and Chloe was, understandably, devastated when her mom died. She was shy and withdrawn for a few years, and that's why I sent her to a therapist. She's resilient though, a tough little cookie who's learning how to adapt.

I love my niece like crazy, and I want to give her the best chance a kid can possibly have. That's why I pay to send her to a school where she's finally thriving, and to do fun activities she enjoys, like photography and art classes, and why I do everything I can to be there for her. That's why the last guy I dated was history after only one month. That was more than a year ago, and Jake didn't understand why Chloe was my priority. "She's not even yours," he'd said. "I wish you'd make time for me the way you do for her."

"Not even a minute, Jake. You won't even get another second."

And Chloe is also why Miller's audition appeals

to me. This new band could be a little extra on
the side.

* * *

I'm humming to myself in Campbell's kitchen the
next day.

He and Miller are picking up last-minute items
for the Christmas party. Even though it's early in
December, Campbell's daughter, Samantha, loves
the holiday so much she's insisted on having two
parties—one early and one later.

Plus, Miller's younger brother, Miles, is in town
for a couple weeks, during a break between his tour
in Australia and a short European leg, where he'll
spend the rest of the month.

Chloe and I grab stools at the kitchen counter.

Samantha loves to bake, and she's enlisted me in
the not-terribly-complex-but-terribly-tempting task
of sprinkling powdered sugar on top of the Nutella
bread pudding.

Chloe leans close and stage-whispers out of the
corner of her mouth, "Want to sneak out with this
one? I'll guard the door while you make a run for it."

I laugh. "I'm one hundred percent in support of
this plan."

"I heard you," Samantha cuts in, in what has to

be her sternest voice possible. "No one is making off with the Christmas goodies."

As she scoops chocolate peanut butter balls from a tray, Mackenzie nods quickly, seconding our plan. "I'll just stuff these peanut butter balls in my bra right now, and then we'll make our escape."

"Patience, ladies, patience," Samantha calls out as she checks the timer on the oven. "Also, under no circumstances are you putting any peanut butter balls in your undergarments."

Mackenzie's eyes widen, and she mimes removing contraband from her pants.

I crack up.

"Just give me a treat. Something to tide me over, then. I'm dying, Sam. Dying, I tell ya," Mackenzie says, swooning dramatically against the counter.

"This is indeed torture of the highest degree," I say, as I sprinkle sugar on the dessert. "You should try doing this without jamming your whole face into the bread pudding."

Samantha swivels around and points a finger accusingly at me. "Do not ruin my Christmas treats. If you do, I will banish you from Samantha's Treat Zone."

I shudder. That sounds like a terrible punishment.

"Say you're sorry, Aunt Ally. I don't want us

banished. Get down on your hands and knees if you have to," Chloe advises in a desperate plea.

I bat my eyes at Samantha. "I promise not to stuff my face into the dessert."

Samantha smiles and nods crisply. "Good. You all deserve a treat now." She doles out chocolate peanut butter balls to each of us, and I moan in pleasure as one melts on my tongue.

As we put the finishing touches on the bread pudding, I find myself humming the audition tune.

Mackenzie cocks her head. "Hey, Ally. What's that you're singing?"

I don't answer right away. I shoot her an impish little grin then wiggle my eyebrows.

"Want to hear something cool?"

Mackenzie and Sam say yes.

I take a deep breath and decide to tell them my good news. I know these ladies well. They're practically family. "You know how Miller finally decided to have auditions to find a new Garfunkel to his Simon?"

They both nod.

I grin, ready to burst. "I submitted an audition, and he went crazy for it."

Mackenzie's eyes flicker like a switch has flipped on. "Oh my God, you must be Honey Lavender!"

"Shh," I say, even though the guys aren't here. I

nod too, pleased that my nom de plume has traveled all the way to Mackenzie's ears.

"He can't stop telling Campbell how psyched he is to hear her sing in person," Mackenzie says.

That intel thrills me. "Here's my plan," I say, then give them the details of what I've been cooking up.

Samantha squeals. "I can't wait to hear how it all goes down."

Later at the party, Miller tugs me aside, a wicked grin on his face. Butterflies take off in a pod race across my entire being. "I found someone amazing to sing with me. She's going to come in to meet with me on Monday."

"That's great," I say, giving my best cool-and-calm-while-I'm-dancing-inside-like-Laura-Linney-in-*Love-Actually* reaction.

"Any chance you can come to the audition, listen to us, and give me some feedback? I'd love your opinion, and it'll be in your studio."

A cough bursts from my throat. My skin flames red hot. Since I haven't yet learned how to clone myself, or spirit-clone myself, for that matter, I give a quick shrug. "I'd love to, but I'm busy then."

He furrows his brow. "But I didn't give you a time."

Oops.

I swallow down a gotcha stone, but then call on my best warrior princess confidence. "I know, silly kitten. I'm busy all day Monday. I have to work on a Casey Stern novel, and the publisher wants me to record at the in-house studios."

He heaves a sigh but then smiles brightly. "I'll ask Miles to join Campbell and me, since he's in town."

He strolls over to his younger brother, and all my nerves crawl up my throat and threaten to throttle me. Now I have to perform my "ta-da, it's me" routine in front of Miller *and* his two brothers.

I could use a spirit clone for sure.

CHAPTER 6

Ally

A little makeup is all a cloned girl needs.

Okay, maybe a wig too. Definitely some sexy clothes.

Fortunately, my brother's wife, Macy, is a genius when it comes to makeup and va-va-voom outfits. She's a makeup artist extraordinaire, and now she's my secret weapon since she's giving me smoldering eyes and pouty lips. The blonde glam wig is perfection too, with its vixen style and bangs that make my eyes a little mysterious as I peek out from under the hair.

But Chloe keeps shaking her head as she gets ready for school on Monday, making peanut butter toast. "Aunt Ally, I don't know how you think you're going to trick Miller."

From my perch at the kitchen counter, I hold up a finger to correct her. "I'm not trying to trick him. I'm trying to get him to see me in a new light."

She shoots me a questioning look. "But he likes your light."

I shake my head as Macy dips into her bag for more makeup. "He likes my light as a friend. I want him to see me as a singer that can match his style."

Chloe shrugs. "I think he likes you for you."

Oh, to be eleven again.

Wait. That sounds awful. Eleven was rough. So was twelve, thirteen, fourteen, and all ages through to seventeen.

"I know he does, but I want him to see me as someone he can sing with."

As she slings her backpack on her shoulder, Chloe looks me over from head to toe. "So, it's like a costume."

I smile, glad that she gets what I'm doing. "Yes! I'm playing a role. I want Miller to see who I can be, and that I'm not *only* the type of woman who can sing 'Amazing Grace,' but I can also sing 'Need You Now' with him, and tunes like 'Love Me Like Crazy.'"

"Good luck, but don't forget Dr. Jane says sometimes you just need to be yourself," Chloe says as she reaches for the door handle. "Bye, Aunt Macy."

"Wait," I call out, then turn to Macy. "I need to walk her to the bus stop on the corner. Be right back."

"Of course. Go."

I pop up, grab a jacket and a scarf, and head down three flights of stairs to take Chloe to the bus stop. Her bus arrives quickly, and I give her a peck on the cheek.

"Bye, Aunt Ally," Chloe says, and it hurts my heart the littlest bit that we're both aunts to her. Yes, Macy has been a part of her life, but I'm the one she lives with, and I take care of her. I've effectively become her mother. Yet at the end of the day, I'm still Aunt Ally to her, and the woman doing my mascara is her aunt too.

And she's my niece.

My niece who I adore.

Even though I love her like a daughter.

"Love you, Monkey. Have an amazing day."

Once she's on the bus, I scurry out of the chilly December air and back to my apartment, where Macy puts the finishing touches on my new look. Like I'm a science fair exhibit, she gestures to me. "Ladies and gentlemen, may I present Honey Lavender, the sultriest of torch singers."

I unzip my sweatshirt and toss it to the floor as she guides me to the full-length mirror in my bedroom. I do look like a woman who fits the name.

The push-up bra Macy told me to wear has lifted the girls higher, while the scoop-neck blouse reveals the curves of said ta-tas. My makeup makes me look all kinds of foxy, with kohl-lined eyes and thick lashes that go on for miles. My red lipstick could stop a truck.

"Damn," I say with a whistle.

"Damn, indeed. And on that note, I need to get my butt back to Brooklyn," Macy says, as she turns around and picks up her makeup bag. "Kirby has to go to work, and I have a newborn to take care of."

"Thanks for coming out here to transform me."

She winks. "You look perfectly sexy and sinful."

She rushes out, and seconds later my phone buzzes with a text from her.

Macy: By the way, you absolutely look like Honey von Trapp.

Ally: Ha! But it's Honey Lavender.

Macy: You do know that sounds like a pen name? You should use that to narrate romance novels.

Ally: I'm trying. But today, I'm trying the costume look.

Macy: Meow, Honey. You should save that get-up for Halloween and go as a sexy . . . anything :)

Ally: Why thank you...I've been looking for an "anything" costume.

Macy: Also, I'm soooooo sorry we're moving. I feel terrible since it's all our fault that you're ditching your Keds for the vamp look.

Ally: Stop! Stop! It's not your fault! This is a huge opportunity for Kirby in Boston, and I will be just fine without the regular sweet-as-pie Zimmerman duo videos.

Macy: You will? *arches skeptical brow*

Ally: I promise. That's why I'm Honey Von Trapping it today. To find the next thing that'll give me little extra pocket money. And because I want to.

Macy: With your pipes and now your smoldering eyes, you're irresistibly sexy and sinful, and I know you'll sound like a million bucks. But maybe try to remember whether you're Honey Von Trapp or Honey Lavender, ya know :)?

Ally: By the way, I picked Lavender for you. Since

you insisted on giving me the lavender streak in the first place.

Macy: And your lavender streak is like a signature of awesome. Love ya, bunches.

I return to the mirror, checking out my side reflection, then my other profile.

I look sinful.

I look hot to trot.

But I also don't look like me.

At all.

Chloe's words echo in my mind. *Be yourself.*

I believe in that. I truly do. But I'm not the singer Miller wants. He wants the woman with the smoky voice, and I need him to see I can be the part.

Except as I stare at myself, my eyes keep darting back to my chest, and the way my breasts look in this top. If I'm drawn to the Boobsy Twins, that's the only place a man will look.

Looking the part is well and good, but I can't entirely play this role. Nor do I want to, I realize. I want to win on my voice and my talent. Not my tits, and not my lipstick.

I tug off the top, toss the push-up bra on my bed,

and change into a regular bra and a simple black sweater that slopes off my shoulder.

There.

I'm leaving something to the imagination.

There's something else that needs to go. This red lipstick is too look-at-me-I'm-Sandra-Dee. I grab a tissue, wipe it off, and slick on some pink lip gloss instead.

I pull on jeans and ankle boots and consider my reflection one more time. I don't look like Honey. I don't look like Ally. I look like a mash-up, and that's what has always served me well: mashing up songs. Today, I'm going to attempt to mash my style with Miller's.

"Wish me luck," I say to my reflection, then I call Campbell and tell him I need a teeny favor in about an hour.

He laughs. "Consider it done."

I leave and head to the studio, telling all these fidgety nerves to get the hell away from me, and don't go near Honey either.

CHAPTER 7

Miller

The eight singers so far have been solid. Some have even bordered on good. The trouble is when you hear a voice that haunts you, and it's a good kind of haunting, nothing else comes close.

"Thanks so much. I'll be in touch," I say to the redheaded alto, Angelica, as she leaves the studio.

I turn to my brothers and Jackson, who asked if he could watch the auditions too, since he's off from school today. Miles dropped off his son, Ben, with our parents for the day. "What do we think, gentlemen?"

Miles shrugs and scratches his stubble-lined jaw. He's working the scruff look hard these days. "I could have taken a nap during that last one." He yawns majestically. "There was no snap, crackle, or pop. No spark that became a fire. No electric—"

"I get it. No chemistry."

"But maybe there will be gobs of it when the next woman comes in," Jackson says.

I stand a little taller. "That's Honey, right?"

Miles scans the list of names then nods. "She's the last one."

Campbell taps his watch then meets my gaze. "Looks like she should be here any minute. Any chance you could grab me a bottle of water?"

I shoot him a look. Campbell isn't usually a can-you-grab-me-a-bottle-of-water type of guy. "Would you like me to order you dinner and set your table too?"

"That sounds nice. Please put me down for a full meal service, as well."

Miles rolls his blue eyes. "I'll go with you, Miller. Our big brother is so lazy sometimes."

I look at Campbell meaningfully, clapping my hand on Miles's shoulder. "See? Dodgeball wants to help me." That's what we've always called Miles, due to his ability to get out of trouble every single time our parents came down on us.

Campbell shoos us out. "I bet those water bottles are so terribly heavy. It's a good thing you have assistance."

Miles and I leave the studio suite and head down the hall.

"You enjoying the break, or are you itching to get back on the road?" I ask him.

"Actually," he says, taking his time answering, "not as much as I thought."

I jerk my gaze toward him. "Touring was always your favorite part of this whole thing."

"It was, and I made it work for a long time, but Ben is starting school soon."

I nod, understanding completely. Miles has hired babysitters and nannies galore for Ben, so his son could be with him on the job in the early years. "You can always tour in summers though."

"That's the plan. Pretty sure I'll go crazy if I don't tour."

"I know the going-crazy feeling well, Dodgeball," I say as I turn into the snack room and grab a couple bottles from the fridge.

"You do know that I have a nickname and you don't, and that's because you're the middle child, and therefore totally unloved."

"I do suffer without love and a nickname," I say wryly as we make our way back to the booth.

I toss a bottle of cold water to Campbell, and he catches it easily then tips his chin toward the glass. "She's in there."

A laser beam of excitement zips through me. "She just arrived?"

"I was a big boy and let her in by myself. She's waiting for you."

I peer through the glass, but she's looking away. Bright blonde hair hits her jaw, showing off the sexy curve of her neck.

Don't think of her neck as sexy, you jackass.

Her neck is functional. It holds up her head.

I uncap the water, take a deep swig, and head into the recording studio.

The second I step inside, I'm walloped by music. There isn't even a moment to extend a hand and say hello. Campbell has already started playing the music track to Lady Antebellum's "Need You Now."

He doesn't usually start it that quickly, so I snap my gaze in his direction, but his head's down. In a split second, Honey launches into the duet, the sweet and sexy notes filling my head like decadent perfume.

I regard her in profile, trying to figure out this blonde in painted-on jeans and boots. She swivels around, and I blink.

The world slows.

My brain blurs.

One of these things is not like the other.

Because there's no way Honey is my best friend.

There's no way that's Ally holding the mic and

singing in a tone I've never heard come from her pipes before.

There's no way her blue eyes are lined that deliciously dark, no way her hair is that sexpot style, no way her lips are so pouty.

My puzzlement shifts from curiosity to intrigue. I've never seen this side of Ally, and I gawk like I'm watching a giraffe dance the rumba at the zoo. She slides into the next verse, lighting me up with her voice.

Her eyes linger on me, roaming over my face. I mouth, *You?* Even though she's here, I still need the confirmation. I still *want* the confirmation.

She nods, smiling playfully as she sings.

I've been tricked. I've been treated. I've been fooled. And I love it.

She sings like a sinner. She sings like an angel. She sounds like whiskey and sugar. I've only ever known her for her church-bell voice, but now she's a glorious mix of dirty and sweet, and I never knew she had it in her.

But I can't marinate in this change-up. It's showtime for me.

Grabbing the mic, I dive into my first line as I gaze into those blue eyes of my friend. Only I have to think of her as Honey, so I sing to the new woman about how I can't do without her, how I need her now.

Something is in the air between us when we sing, something charged. Something that hasn't been there before. Stage chemistry.

I move closer as if I'm drawn by the pull of gravity that I have no control over. We lock eyes and everyone else fades away. I'm still in shock that I'm loving singing a song with my best friend.

That's what terrifies me. Especially since we sound good together, and we move well together.

Maybe we even look good together, as we belt out this hot-as-fuck duet, and for the first time we're not butchering a holiday tune or destroying "Total Eclipse of the Heart" at karaoke. As she moves closer to me, we sing the final chorus like it's going out of style, and when the music softens, I can't resist. I finger a strand of her blonde wig, the coconut scent from her lotion floating into my nose.

Reluctantly, I let the hair fall.

Clapping rings loud in my ears.

Jackson, Miles, and Campbell give a standing O. Jackson holds up his phone, pointing to it, letting me know he caught it on video.

"Chemistry," the guys all shout, practically in unison.

But I'm not supposed to have chemistry with my best friend.

That's the problem.

"What the hell just happened here?" I whisper to Ally, befuddled.

Her mouth opens, and her eyes go wide, and she blurts out, "I have an appointment. I need to go."

She takes off, leaving in her wake a trail of chemistry and coconut and confusion.

CHAPTER 8

Miller

"Don't just stand here!" Miles gestures wildly to the door. "Go after her."

But my feet stay planted as my brain tries to process the new side of Ally. "But she said she had an appointment."

Campbell guffaws. "She's your best friend, and she just took off like her ass was on fire. Follow her."

Jackson gestures to the door too. "Listen to your elder and listen to the younger people who know best. Go!"

I'm not even sure what to say, or if Ally's upset, but I do what they tell me, bolting from the studio, scanning the hall for the woman in the blonde wig.

Or maybe I should be looking for Ally's brunette hair with that bright purple streak. Maybe she's yanked off the wig, tossed it in the trash can, darted down an alley, and started climbing up the walls, parkour-style. Or maybe I've seen too many movies.

Either way, I rush to the lobby of Platinum Sky and ask the receptionist where Ally went. The kind lady with huge glasses and a happy-to-help grin points to the elevator. "She went *thataway*."

And now we're both living in a comic book panel.

I step into the elevator, stab the G button, and will the lift to move faster. Maybe Ally thinks I'm upset with her?

When I reach the ground floor, I blast by security and out to the street to find Ally standing against the building in the brisk December air, bent at the waist, breathing heavily.

Concern threads through me. I reach for her elbow, and she flinches when I touch her. "Are you okay?"

She waves her hand in front of her, still hunched over. "Needed to get some air." Her voice comes out soft and a little squeaky.

"Are you sure?"

She nods then lifts her face, the blue eyes I know so well peeking out at me from underneath her vampy wig like Charlize Theron in *Atomic Blonde*. "Are you mad at me?" she asks in that sweet soprano.

I laugh and shake my head. "No. Why the hell would I be mad at you?"

Her eyes are nervous. "I was worried you'd think I tricked you."

I rub my hand on her back, and she straightens. "Even if you had sent in an audition tape in full costume with a prosthetic nose and colored contacts and who knows what else, I wouldn't be mad. In fact, I'd probably think that was awesome. What you did was totally ballsy."

A hint of a smile appears. "Yeah?"

"Also, for the record, you can pull tricks on me any time because it will literally never bother me."

She laughs lightly and takes a deep breath, then swallows and meets my eyes. "Sorry I took off. Everything hit me when we finished singing, and I needed to breathe."

I narrow my eyes and study her, as if I'm conducting a full appraisal. "Chest moving up and down. Air coming in and out. Check. Your oxygen intake system seems functional now."

"Did you hate it?" Her voice rises as she asks the question, laced with nerves.

I scoff, surprised she'd even think that. "No. I thought you were incredible. I was just kind of shocked that it was you. And I was shocked that we actually sounded decent together."

That smile of hers widens, occupying as much

real estate as it possibly can on her face. "You thought we sounded good together?"

"We had chemistry out the wazoo. Hell, we had it out the kazoo. But what did you think?"

"Of our 'zoos?"

I nod, laughing.

She shakes her head, her sunshine-blonde hair moving perfectly in tandem with her. She shrugs then nods.

"Yes, no, maybe?" I ask, trying to translate her sign language.

"It was hard for me to focus on anything but staying in character. I didn't think you'd even want to listen if it was just me."

My brow creases. "Just *you*?"

She stares me down. "You've made it clear you thought we sounded terrible together."

"It wasn't unfounded. You've heard the way we sang 'Santa Claus Is Comin' to Town.'"

"That's why I wanted to show you I could sing in another style. I wanted to show you what I'm capable of. That's why I had to audition as someone else—for you to take me seriously."

Understanding flicks on like a light bulb. It blares so brightly, I nearly squint. Ally doesn't want to sing with me for kicks. She needs this gig.

My heart goes heavy as concrete in my chest. I want to help her, but I don't want to lose her. I don't know how to have both Ally the friend and Ally the bandmate. The first band I played with after the Heartbreakers broke up was a disaster. I started Candid Bandits with my best buddy from college on guitar and me on keyboards. Craig and I knocked out three good tunes before we started butting heads on everything. And I mean every-damn-thing: the style, the practice schedule, the distro plans. We could never get on the same page. I kept making suggestions, but eventually, he let loose and said I was a know-it-all. *"You think you know everything because you were in a band before. So what? Things are different now."*

And they were different two weeks later, when he quit and ditched our friendship too.

From Craig to Tiffany, the writing is on the wall. I don't play well with friends.

"Ally," I say softly. "Of course I take you seriously, but do you really think we should form a duo together?"

Her expression falls, morphing from adrenaline-fueled excitement to fresh disappointment. "You don't? I thought you liked how I sang as Honey."

"I loved it. But I don't want to lose you as a friend."

She stares at me as if I'm speaking Turkish. "How would you lose me as a friend by singing with me?"

"You know what happened with Craig?" I ask,

reminding her, since I'm pretty sure Ally knows all my stories. She knows about the Tiffany debacle too. "That's what worries me. My best bud from college is persona non grata. The drummer I dated slaughtered my Xbox. It seems easy to play or sing together with a friend, but then you have to agree on so many things that are more important than whether you want to see *Love, Simon* or *Ready Player One*."

She whispers, "*Love, Simon*."

I whisper back, "*Ready Player One*." Then I sigh. "That's my point. It's like going into business with your bud. Everyone thinks it's a good idea on the surface. But what happens when you disagree? Or you want to go in different directions?"

"How did you deal with it when it was your brothers?" she asks, with an earnestness that nearly breaks me.

Because they're my brothers, I want to say. *Because we're family.* That's the difference—they're stuck with me. She has the choice to ditch me anytime. "Because when I was a dick, they couldn't disown me. I can't bear the thought that you'd realize I'm really an asshole to work with. And I am. I'm a total asshole as a bandmate."

She quirks up the corners of her lips, but it's not a smile. It's more like she's trying to make sense of me. "And you don't want me to be exposed to the butthead side of you?"

"Yes," I say, pleading. "If we play together, something could happen to our friendship."

She seems to fasten on a smile. "I get it."

"I'm sorry." I reach for her shoulder, squeezing it.

She side-eyes my hand. "Miller," she says, in that voice women use when they're going to put men in their place. "This isn't an *I'm sorry* moment. We're all good."

"I feel bad though."

"Don't worry about it. I don't need apology balloons or even an apology at all."

I snort, when she mentions the lame-ass gift her ex-boyfriend Tyler gave her last year when he was two hours late to see *Matilda* with her and Chloe, and they'd missed the show. Ally won't tolerate hurting, disappointing, or just plain dismissing Chloe. "As if I would ever get you apology balloons."

She smiles. "Good. Balloons are bad for wildlife. Besides, you didn't do anything wrong. Also"—she purses her lips then casts a glance down the street —"I really do have to go."

This time I don't chase her down.

Because I lied.

I'm not an asshole. Please. I'm a cuddly teddy bear.

But I also know how business works.

It works best with family. It works best with acquaintances. I'm jonesing to play again in a band, but that's because I miss working with other musicians. I miss being part of a business team.

But a business team isn't a playground for friends. Or for lovers.

If you get too close to either, the next thing you know, your Xbox is splattered on Fifth Avenue.

I can buy a new Xbox fifty times over, but I can't buy a new friendship.

CHAPTER 9

Ally

Macy: Give me the 411. Was he so blown away by Honey Lavender that he said, "Please, play sweet music with me now"?

Ally: Hardly. He's freaking out. He thinks we can't be friends and sing together.

Macy: Well, that may be true. Look what happened to the White Stripes.

Ally: Could you have picked a worse example than a husband and wife team that had all sorts of issues?

Macy: I'm just saying even the Righteous Brothers split up.

Ally: And one of them died of cocaine-related heart trouble. What else could go wrong?

Macy: You could be Sonny and Cher. Or worse—Ike and Tina.

Ally: I feel super uplifted right now.

Macy: Even Simon and Garfunkel can't stick together. Those guys keep doing reunions then breaking up.

Ally: Why don't you make a list and put it in an email?

Macy: Who has time for that? Taylor Swift and John Mayer, Katy Perry and John Mayer . . . wait. You're fine, as long as you don't sing a duet with John Mayer.

Ally: Duly noted. I'll stay away from him.

Macy: Also, why are you bringing up couples who sang and then split? Are you and Miller a couple and you haven't told me? Tell me, tell me, tell me.

Ally: We're not a couple. And it's totally fine if he doesn't want to sing together. I auditioned, I put my best foot forward, and now I'm going to focus on the things I can control. Like weather and the national debt.

Macy: I'm sorry, honey. I know you wanted to pull this off. But, joking aside, when people go into business with their friends, it can blow up.

Ally: Maybe it was crazy to try to push our friendship into some other category.

Macy: I used to think that about Kirby.

Ally: I'm covering my ears when you talk about MY BROTHER who you fell for. Some friend. ☺

Macy: I couldn't help falling for my bestie's brother. He's wonderful, and so are you. And Miller is just being cautious about the band thing. Don't let it get you down.

Ally: I'm not even thinking about Miller's band anymore. Not one bit. Not one stinking iota.

CHAPTER 10

Miller

Jackson is pacing the hall as I turn the corner past the receptionist's desk.

I rake a hand through my hair, trying to figure out what the hell to do with the spectacular mess my plans have become. Jackson's face is lit up though, and he points to his phone. "Miller, man, you need to see this."

"I do?" I ask half-heartedly.

"I have this kick-ass editing software on my phone. I put a clip together in ten minutes." He's practically bouncing as he goes into the recording studio, looking back to make sure I'm following. I do and flop down in a wheeled chair between my brothers, rolling back into the wall with a thud.

Jackson brandishes his phone dramatically and hits play.

The first screen is a title card. *Break it Down.*

I arch a brow.

"Wait for it," he assures me.

The screen reads, *Go BTS for the making of a brand-new musical duo.*

"BTS?"

"Behind the scenes," he answers quickly. "I'll spell it out next time. Keep watching."

The next clip is a shot of Jackson strolling down the hall of the studio, talking to the camera, selfie-style.

"Ever wonder what goes into forming a band in the era of YouTube, Spotify, digital everything, and the new musical world order? I'm going to take you behind the scenes into the inner workings of . . ." He stops at the door of the studio, pauses, then stage-whispers, "Hashtag ZimmerHart."

I raise my eyebrows. Is he joking? But then the camera zooms in on Ally and me, and my eyes are drawn to the screen. Damn, she is luscious as Honey.

Note to self: don't think dirty thoughts about your best friend.

But hell, that body, that face, that wig. The way she looked. How she smelled.

I scoot back in the chair, like a slight change in position will shift matters away from my pants.

Enough, brain. Focus. Just fucking focus.

I wipe the filth from the gray matter and slap on blinders, zeroing in only on the tunes.

Except I didn't realize we were that close when we sang.

Ally's inches away from me, and the look on her face is seductive and sensual. Why the hell did I pick *that* tune to sing today? What was I thinking choosing a sexy song of desire?

I tug at my collar, my temperature ticking up a few degrees as I watch the small screen, wishing my brothers and Jackson were gone, wishing I was alone to enjoy this.

I mean, study this.

I want to study this video.

Understand it.

Because it's like watching a foreign film without subtitles. I don't know what's going on, so I have to rely on the actions, and the actions make one thing clear—we're setting the studio on fire. We're giving off fumes of lust.

I blink, trying to make sense of what I'm seeing.

It must be the song. Must be that it's a great sexy duet, and we were both getting into the meaning and the lyrics.

That's the way it should be.

Jackson touches the screen with a satisfied flourish, an expectant look in his dark eyes. "What do you think? This might be a crazy idea, but as soon as you two started singing, I knew I was witnessing something I could use for my scholarship application."

I crease my brow. "What? How?"

"My submission for the media scholarship."

Awareness slams into me like a truck. He's mentioned needing to submit a short documentary for the scholarship he's applying for.

"*This* would be your submission? Hashtag ZimmerHart?"

"You don't have to keep that name."

"But it's a fun one," Miles jumps in. "Also, you'd be helping your little brother, and I don't mean me, because I'm beyond help."

I laugh at Miles's goofball side. "True. You're a lost cause," I say, smacking his shoulder.

Jackson looks at me, all puppy dog eyes. "If you don't want me to shoot it, that's cool, but I stitched this together hoping it would convince you. I was looking at the requirements for the scholarship, and the main thing is to submit your own documentary. I thought this would be an awesome thing to show a behind-the-scenes look into how your duo comes together."

Campbell meets my gaze, tilting his forehead

toward Jackson. "That's a smart idea for a scholar-ship app, Miller."

I heave a sigh. "Let's be honest here. What are the chances this is going to work out with Ally? I'm not close with anyone I've played with except you two dweebs, and you have to like me."

Campbell crinkles his nose. "Wait. You think we like you?"

"Fuck off," I say.

Miles raises his eyebrows. "Don't swear in front of your little bro."

Jackson rolls his eyes. "Guys."

Miles taps his chest. "Hey, I meant me."

Campbell rises from his chair and plants a hand on my shoulder. "It's up to you, Miller. But I thought you were always the most optimistic. And now you're worried it won't work out if you sing with Ally when you haven't even started? You and Ally are tight, and I can't see anything splitting you up. Maybe do it temporarily?"

Miles snaps his fingers. "Try it for a month. Jam together, write some songs, make some videos. Do it DIY-style. Post them online. Let Jackson film it and see how it goes." Miles claps his hands together like a coach. "And let's get this dude the scholarship he deserves."

The scales weigh heavily on one side. Jackson

needs a scholarship. Ally needs a little extra money. I need . . . someone to sing with.

That someone isn't going to be either of the guys I share blood with, so maybe they're right. Maybe it needs to be Ally-turned-Honey.

Maybe a set time frame will keep this from exploding. As I noodle on the idea of a temporary arrangement, my heart rate slows to normal. Short-term is my middle name.

I mean, I'm excellent at striking temporary deals to sing with my best friend.

Miles smacks my knee. "Just talk to Ally. See if that would work for her."

But the thing is, I don't think I have to talk to Ally. She's pretty much all in, and this is entirely up to me.

I just need to make sure I don't fuck it up.

Taking a breath, I begin to formulate a plan.

CHAPTER 11

Ally

"The clock ticked ever closer to the day of reckoning, and she promised she'd be ready to reclaim her empire and to pounce on the enemy for daring to challenge her birthright."

I take a breath and finish my work for the day on the Kiersten White–style historical epic, with a heroine so badass she doesn't have a moment to wallow in dreams not coming true. Not when heads are rolling in the courts of yesteryear.

After I leave the in-house production studio, I find the audio manager waiting for me in a hallway lined with framed movie-poster-size images of the publishing house's most popular titles. A gleam of pride flickers inside me—I narrated three of those ten. The last one is adjacent to a framed image of a new TV show the house's sister network launched last year, with the rest of the TV pictures extending down the wall.

Angie waggles her fingers at me. "I heard a little bit of your work today. The battle scene was chilling." She shudders as if recalling the multiple impalements suffered on the battlefield, *Game of Thrones*–style. Her blue eyes are big and sparkly behind her rhinestone-studded glasses.

"Teens in the middle ages give new meaning to the word fierce. I almost felt like I was back in those days, though I'm glad I'm not. Only partly because of the risk of beheading."

She laughs. "As am I. Both because of the beheading, and because I can't give up my modern conveniences." She winks. "Like my e-reader or my smartphone."

"Ditto," I say as we head to the elevator. I adjust my ponytail. I loved that blonde wig, but having my natural dark color feels more . . . me. I returned to my regular hairdo after leaving Miller this morning. The wig is tucked neatly at the bottom of my purple purse.

Angie hits the down button at the bank of elevators and says she'll see me tomorrow. But before she can trot back to her desk, she swivels around, smacking her forehead. "I almost forgot to tell you. I know you're eager to try new genres, so I've been looking into some potential new projects for you. Hoping something will work out soon."

I mentally cross my fingers, but play it cool. "That all sounds good to me. Looking forward to mixing it up."

Angie smiles slyly. "I'll keep you posted."

As I zip down to the main floor, I count off how much time I have before I need to pick up Chloe from her photography class—about an hour and a half. It's a cold day, but I have my new purple mittens and a matching hat, so maybe I'll walk home from Midtown to Chelsea for the extra exercise. The cold air always clears my head.

I need to return to the right zone before I talk to Miller again. The friendship zone, that is. I need to let go of the idea that we might have played well together.

But when I step outside, Miller's waiting. He looks like a dog wearing a dog shaming sign. He actually holds up his phone, and the screen reads: *This isn't an apology balloon.*

I chuckle. "I told you. No apology balloons necessary."

"And see? I listened." That grin of his isn't tooth-paste-commercial ready. It's sheepish, but it also says he has a secret.

He must, or why would he be standing in the middle of Midtown on a crisp winter day with the phone sign in one hand and a honey bear and a bottle of lotion in the other? "Who is your friend? Also, how did you know where I was?" I point to the skyscraper where the publisher is housed, right across from Rockefeller Center and its huge, lit Christmas tree overseeing the ice rink.

"You said you had a Casey Stern book to work on, so I looked up her publisher, and she's with Butler Press. Ergo, *you* would be at Butler Press, and I figured you'd be done."

I give a low whistle. "Impressive detective work." The fact that he's here makes me feel hopeful I didn't push our friendship beyond what it could handle. "Hey, we're all good. Let's just move on. Whoever you sing with, I'm sure they will be amazing. And you know I'll be your biggest fan."

I flash him a bright smile, and I feel it inside me too. This morning was such a small blip in the history of our friendship—I won't let it change a damn thing.

He takes a beat, shuffles his feet, and tilts his head. "But what if I didn't want you to be my biggest fan?"

He stuffs his phone into his pocket then hands me the lotion. It's lavender-scented. He thrusts the honey bear at me next. I put two and two together and catch my breath at the possibility he's had a change of heart.

"Miller," I say slowly, as a pack of men in business suits and trench coats march past us, heads bent over their smartphones. "Are you saying . . .?"

He nods, his familiar smile returning to its rightful place. "Do you want to be Hashtag ZimmerHart?"

I laugh in the middle of Fifth Avenue as rush-hour crowds race by. "Yes, but that's the worst name ever for a band."

"Worse than Savory Gerbils?"

I crinkle my nose, as I drop the honey bear and the lotion into my purse. "You have me there. Also, please tell me there isn't a band called that?"

He shudders. "No, but there almost was."

"Spill."

"Once upon a time, Miles had a pair of pet gerbils when he was eight. He used to joke that he was going to start his own band and name it for his gerbils, Sweet and Savory. When he joined us, we told him we'd let him into the band, but only if we could change the name to the Gerbils."

I smirk in delight at the tale of their brotherly antics. "What did he say?"

"He said he'd be fine with that, but he preferred we called ourselves the Savory Gerbils. He passed the test of loyalty, so we let him in."

"And to think the Heartbreakers might have been called the Savory Gerbils."

"Or we could be, since you hate Hashtag ZimmerHart." Miller frowns dramatically.

"I despise it the way a rogue princess despises warring clans who threaten her homeland." I straighten my spine, neat and tall. "A new name it shall be," I say, like I'm royally decreeing.

He rubs his palms together. "All right, let's get cracking on names." He stares at the sky as if in thought, and as he does, I take a moment to let the reality sink in. We're doing this. He changed his mind. I'm going to sing with my best friend. I nearly break out into a tap-dance, Gene Kelly "Singin' in the Rain"–style.

"Do you want to be the Apology Balloon Buddies instead?" Miller asks.

Laughing, I shake my head. "No. But what made you change your mind? I thought you were worried earlier about our friendship."

His expression turns serious. "I was. I am. But then I watched the video of us singing, and we looked good together."

"I want to see that."

He grabs his phone and swipes the screen, showing me a few seconds. "Damn," I whistle, as I watch how I sashayed and sidled right up to him. I tap my finger to my tongue then the screen, and make a sizzling sound.

He closes the clip. "Jackson wants to make a mini doc of us forming a band for his scholarship submission for a media program. It should pay a big chunk of his school if he nabs it."

I bounce on my toes. "That sounds like an amazing opportunity."

"It is. I'm psyched for him. But I'm psyched for us too, if we can do this right. I figure if we're mature and thoughtful, we can make it work. Do you want to try it for a month? Like a test run? What's the worst that can happen in a month?"

I'm a glass-half-full person, so I turn his words around. "Or what's the best that can happen in a month?"

He squares his shoulders. "Honey Lavender, do you want to sing with me?"

I throw my arms around him and say yes. He hugs me back, and I inhale his woodsy scent, sharpened by the cold and smelling more delicious than a friend of mine should rightfully smell.

I shouldn't linger on how yummy Miller smells, but I'm so damn excited I don't care. I inhale one more happy lungful of him before my boots sink down to the sidewalk.

"I guess you're excited."

I hold up a thumb and forefinger. "A little."

He rubs his hands together. "Let's get cracking. Since Savory Gerbils, Balloon Buddies, and Hashtag ZimmerHart are out, want to discuss better names and rules of engagement?"

My eyes drift to Rockefeller Center. "I have thirty minutes before I need to head downtown. Let's do three things at once."

CHAPTER 12

Ally

Fifteen minutes later, I've laced up a pair of skates, and so has Miller.

As we circle around the ice rink, we decide we'll tackle a few originals, with him doing most of the writing, since he's quick and fast. Plus, he has some songs he's been working on for a few months, and he'll put the finishing touches on them to suit our duet style. I'll plan some covers and secure rights for us to sing those online and on stage. If it all goes well, we'll try to land a gig soonish. Time is of the essence, so we'll squeeze in recording sessions quickly.

"This is easy," I say, gesturing with my mittened

hands as we glide and talk, since we both can hold our own on skates. "All we have to do is remember that our friendship comes first. Above all else."

"Does that mean we agree that if we disagree, we'll remain friends?"

I laugh as we glide past a family of four, skating in a row like ducks. "Sort of. But we also agree to talk things through. To be adults. We don't throw video game controllers from windows, or stomp off like children."

Miller nods like he's processing this information, as we weave around some teenagers taking selfies. "And we have that time limit," he adds. "We'll see how it goes for a month and then regroup."

"Exactly. We have the rules of engagement in place. It's like in a novel where the hero and heroine agree to a thirty-day arrangement and then walk away."

He shoots me a curious look as we skate. "That happens in young adult books?"

"It's more common in romance. Let's say the heroine is a little inexperienced and wants some lessons in seduction. They might agree to thirty days of sexual education. Or maybe they both have issues from the past and don't want commitment, so they agree to a month-long deal. Or maybe they're friends but want to scratch an itch, so they lay out the rules of the road."

Miller digs his blades in to stop, grabs the side of the rink, and doubles over. "To scratch an itch?"

I laugh too, as I stop next to him. "Yes, sometimes friends get horny for each other in romance novels."

"If we get hot to trot, do we outline the rules of the horny road?"

I swat him, because it's easier than dealing with the little zing in my chest when he says *hot to trot* in reference to us. "We're singing together, not making out."

His expression turns deadly serious. "Promise me something, Ally."

"Yes?"

He sets a hand on my shoulder and takes a deep breath. "If you ever want lessons in seduction from a friend, please come to me."

I roll my eyes, doing my best to make light of his suggestion, even though a part of me knows he'd be the first person I'd ask. Except I don't think I need or want lessons in seduction, even though it's been a while for me. "Yes, Miller. I'll come to you with ribbons and a request to try various positions. But only if you answer the door freshly showered and wearing just a towel."

He pretends to consider it, then nods. "That's a deal," he says, offering a hand to shake.

I take it, and he growls in appreciation, a sexy, husky noise I've never heard from him before. The sound tangoes over my skin, and unexpected tingles zip over my chest. The sensation surprises me, like someone jumped out from behind a door. But then I try to reason it through. When I narrate battle scenes, my heart often pounds harder. It's not unreasonable I'd have a physical reaction to this kind of vaguely dirty back-and-forth.

"Ribbons and Positions. Can that be our name?"

I screw up the corner of my lips, thinking. "Positions with Ribbons?"

"Other Uses for Ribbons?" he posits, and I giggle. Because it's honestly not a bad name.

"That's a little bit naughty."

He brings his face closer to mine, like he did when we sang. "You're a little naughty when you're Honey."

Heat unfurls in me, spreading from my chest to my arms. *Normal reaction*, I remind myself. It doesn't mean anything at all, so I keep going with it, volleying the flirting ball right back at him. "You're naughty when I'm Honey."

He whispers a hoarse, "*I know.*"

I swallow roughly, and before the moment veers into another kind of thirty-day arrangement that would be far too dangerous for either one of us, I push off, skating again. "C'mon, friend," I say, emphasizing the role he plays in my life.

We've been friends for six years, and it's hard to

imagine anything getting in the way of that, even playing music together.

We met at a retro arcade in Brooklyn one evening. He saw me kicking butt on Donkey Kong and recognized me from my YouTube videos.

During a break in my game, he introduced himself and told me how much he enjoyed the Zimmerman Duo, especially our performance of "Somewhere Over the Rainbow." Naturally, that delighted me. I'm not spotted often, and I'd liked it coming from someone like him, since I was familiar with his success as a Heartbreaker.

He'd returned to his game of Joust but was failing miserably at it. I've always been good at arcade games, so I gave him a few pointers and then showed him what to do to reach the next level.

He followed my tips and was successful.

The funny thing is, I felt a little spark that first night, especially when he thrust his arms up in victory, wrapped me in a hug of thanks, and asked me if I wanted to grab a beer.

I'd been tempted to act on that spark. To slide in next to him on his side of the table. To flirt and then some. But I had a crystal-clear vision of what would happen if I did.

I saw us hooking up, kissing hot and heavy. I saw me inviting him to my place and us spending the night tangled up together.

I'd thought of Lindsay, home with her daughter. I wasn't worried about an accidental pregnancy, per se. But I was worried about never seeing Miller again, like Lindsay never saw Chloe's dad again.

Miller and I got along so well I knew right away I wanted him in my life. I didn't want to risk losing him to the end of a fling. I liked him so much as a person that whatever flicker of attraction I felt, I forced out of my mind, sweeping it away.

"Do you want to be friends?" I'd asked him.

He'd flinched, like he was taken aback, coughing on his beer. But then he'd nodded. "Yeah. Let's do this again."

I've seen him through girlfriends; he's seen me through boyfriends. We've leaned on each other through heartache and heartbreak, sorrow and joy, side by side.

Miller helped me through my own grief when my sister died, and then he rose to the occasion over the years, helping Chloe whenever he could. All because we made a choice years ago to put friendship first.

Of course, I don't know if he felt the same spark I did that night at the arcade, so perhaps it was easy as pie for him to keep me in the friend zone.

It's mostly easy for me to keep him there, except for moments like this. Like now, when my heart races in overdrive, and my hormones remind me they want attention now and then.

But there's too much on the line to give in. I have bills, and work, and a kid to raise. She's my focus, and she's why I wanted to do this in the first place.

We skate and review the plan to write and record, since Jackson will be shooting videos of our sessions for his documentary. All we have to do is not be jerks, we decide.

He holds out his hand and we shake. Happiness spreads through me, and I love how this day has worked out, so I spin around on my skates and issue a challenge. "Catch me if you can."

I take off around the ice, but soon enough, he picks up speed and flies past me. His arm darts out as if he's going to grab my waist, but I don't fall.

He does.

Flat on his ass, the side of his head whacking the ice.

My heart hammers as I jam the blade of my skate into the ice, stopping in a spray. Quickly, I bend down next to him. He's flat as a board, head against the ice, blades up.

"Are you okay?" I ask, visions of concussions and bruises haunting me.

"I'm wounded," he mutters.

"What's wounded?" I ask as I look him over from head to toe. He's wearing jeans and a sweater and—wait.

His belly is moving up and down.

He's laughing. The fucker is laughing.

He clutches his chest, moaning. "It's my pride though. It's never going to be the same."

I straighten, shaking my head in amusement. "Male pride is so fragile."

"You're telling me. Can you see if I can get a new shipment of it?"

I tap my mitten against my lips. "I'm pretty sure all the stores are closed, and Amazon doesn't offer Prime shipping for that product."

His lips curve up into a grin, and that's when I spot a slight bruise on his cheek. Instinctively, I reach out, yanking off my mittens and brushing my thumb across the wound.

When I touch him, he startles, but then sighs as I check out the small mark. "You do have a little scrape here. I think you hurt your cheek."

"Will I live?" He turns his face to me, and his eyes pin mine. There's something in those hazel eyes I haven't seen before. A flicker of heat, perhaps. A wink of desire.

I shiver, forcing myself to look away, because his eyes are doing something to me. They're sending my thermometer higher than it should be, like when we were in the studio singing to each other. I felt that spark then in my toes, in my fingertips, and in the center of my body.

"You'll survive." I reach for his hand. He looks down at my fingers, locking with his.

"Are you going to pull me?"

"Of course. You fell."

He shakes his head, sitting straight up. "I will have zero manly pride then." He wobbles slightly, then stands, holding his arms out wide. "See? Machismo restored."

He grabs my palm and then skates with me, holding hands.

That shiver returns. And it's not from the chilly air. It's from Miller. From these naughty comments he's always made, which feel a little different now. I do my best to talk myself out of it since we've always been a little flirty, a little playful.

But when we reach the skate stand and he slowly lets go of my hand, he looks at me that way again.

The trouble is there's a new fire in my body that doesn't feel particularly friendly either. I do my best to dismiss it.

But it's under my skin.

CHAPTER 13

Miller

When it comes to nightmares, I'm familiar with the standard repertoire.

You've got "Teeth Falling Out," a classic. *Shudder.*

There's "Back in High School Having Forgotten Everything I Ever Knew about the War of 1812," a horror that hits a little too close to reality.

And, of course, "Naked on Stage." Though, oddly, considering the amount of time I've spent on stage, I've never had that one.

But nothing compares to the line at the Office of Public Records.

Jackson's mom lost his birth certificate in an apartment fire a few years ago. He needs it for the scholarship application, so about a century ago, I brought him here to order a copy.

Fine, maybe we've been waiting more like twenty-eight minutes, but I'm eager to get back to songwriting, something I've been doing every night at my piano for the last several days—fine-tuning the songs I've had in my back pocket.

At twenty-nine minutes, we make it to the front, where Jackson requests the duplicate. The bedraggled clerk, strands of hair slipping from her bun, pops a Skittle between bubble-gum-pink-colored lips, then taps the details out on her keyboard. She reaches for another candy, then frowns, forlorn, at the empty bag.

"What's your favorite color of Skittle?" I inquire.

She looks up and blinks in slow-motion, as if not sure who I'm asking. "I like the red ones best. But the purple ones are pretty tasty too."

"I heard a story the other day that all Skittles actually taste the same," I say. Jackson gives me a look like I've started talking to a houseplant. "Maybe"—I pause to read her name tag—"Beverly feels that way too."

She tilts her head and scratches her jaw. "Huh. I always thought they tasted different."

"So do I. But somebody did a test, and apparently, it's really the same flavor."

"That's crazy. I know the green tastes like lime," Jackson says.

I give him a serious look. "But do you really? Or do you just *think* it tastes like lime? That's the question."

Slowly, as if it's the first time in ages, Beverly smiles. "Do you think it's like the Matrix, and we're all experiencing a programmed reality?"

I widen my eyes. "Maybe that's why they don't make blue Skittles, just red ones. So we have to stay in the Matrix."

Beverly slaps the counter, cackling so loud that heads turn across the musty records office. "That must be it." She returns to the computer screen and says, "I can have that copy ready for you on Monday."

Jackson sighs. "We have to come back?"

She looks sympathetic. "Either that or I can mail it to you, and it'll arrive in a week."

He turns to me. "The application isn't due until right before Christmas, but I need to get the preliminary paperwork filed next week to be eligible. Only, I have to take my grandpa to the doctor after school on Monday."

"Can your dad pick it up for you?" Beverly suggests, meaning me.

I laugh. "I'm just a friend. But I can definitely pick it up for him if that's allowed."

"You can do that. We just need you both to sign a form, granting permission." She slides a piece of paper to us that we both sign.

Jackson smiles. "Thanks, man. I owe you."

I wave a hand. "It's nothing." I grin at Beverly. "I'll bring the Skittles."

She laughs then beckons for me to lean closer as she whispers, "Come at 12:35. I return from my lunch then, but the office doesn't reopen till 12:45. We'll get you in and out quickly."

"You're a goddess, Beverly."

She smiles, and Jackson says thank you.

As we take the hallway to the exit, Jackson looks at me as if I'm wearing a cape and rippling with muscles. Well, I do have muscles.

"Dude. That was majestic." He holds up a palm for a high-five, and I deliver. "Did you do that with the Skittles to get a better appointment?"

I shake my head, laughing. "No. I had no idea she'd be so cool. I just like making conversation."

"With anyone?"

"Think about how her day must be—cranky people asking the same thing over and over. It's as easy to strike up a conversation as stand there staring at my phone, and nicer for everyone."

"You are the master."

"Tell that to my mom. When I was a kid, she said

she couldn't get me to shut up, so I'm glad someone finally appreciates my gift for gab."

"I definitely appreciate it," he says as we reach the door. "When do you go back in the studio again so I can start recording? I'm antsy to make some videos."

"Tomorrow," I tell him, and I'm fired up for Jackson. Watching this kid grow from a boy to a man over the last ten years has been an incomparable joy. He's learned to navigate a world that's been merciless to him and his family. He's tackled it with his camera and his wits, and now he's just steps away from being the first in his family to go to college.

I'm fired up for other reasons too. I cannot wait to start making new music again. For the last week, since we decided to duet together, Ally and I have been planning our song list and writing some new ones, and already I feel invigorated.

But there's more. A reason I haven't made sense of yet.

I'm excited for the chance to get up close to Ally again. Maybe to dance together, to see how our chemistry plays out the second time. To look into her eyes, and to feel that wild spark.

I want that for the sake of the music, of course.

Not because my heart was on fire when she sang sweet dirty words to me from inches away.

Once we're back in the city, I say goodbye to

Jackson and head to Dr. Insomnia's to meet Ally and Chloe.

Note to self: don't let on you just thought about how Ally's lush body would feel pressed against you.

Dammit. Now I'm thinking about how she'd feel pressed against me naked.

The answer?

Spectacular.

Maybe I need a red Skittle to enter an artificial reality where I'm not inappropriately attracted to my best friend.

CHAPTER 14

Ally

At Dr. Insomnia's, I study the close-up image of the chalk-covered sidewalk.

"This is Washington Square Park?"

Chloe nods. "Can you tell where I took this from?"

I peer more closely at the image on her laptop, where she's showing me the pictures she shot and edited for her photography class. Then, a burst of clarity. "You shot the picture from the ground, right?"

She wiggles her eyebrows, like a delighted cartoon character. "The teacher challenged us to work on different and unusual angles. I went down on my belly and took the picture from there."

My smile widens. "Brilliant. That's a fantastic approach, and I love that it makes me think about the park in a new way."

She clicks to the next one. It's a close-up of a water pipe in black-and-white, with a drop of water falling from the opening. "It has a very spooky feel. Is that what you were going for?"

She thrusts a victorious fist into the air, shouting *yes*. "That's exactly what I was going for," she says at a more normal volume.

"Do you like taking pictures of spooky stuff?"

"I like shooting weird things. Different things. I like finding new angles. When we were taking pictures in the park, I did a super close-up on an empty swing at the swing set." With the lightning speed of Generation iPad, she flicks through her photos to find the swing in question.

In the image, she's zeroed in on the chains of the swing as it twists in the wind.

It's evocative and unusual, but it's definitely creepy. Enough that I wonder—is this a sign that Chloe has issues? Is she trying to tell me something? I'm no expert on parenting, but my approach with Chloe has always been to be direct. To talk to her. To ask her.

I lean on that. "Level with me. Should I be worried that you're taking pictures of creepy things?"

"You think I'm going to go even more emo on you?"

I laugh lightly. "I'm a little worried."

"I thought about it," she says, drily. "But I decided I'm done with the emo phase. I'm going to work on my Wendy phase."

I furrow my brow, laughing still. "What is a Wendy phase?"

"Aren't all happy girls named Wendy?" She taps her chin. "Well, that girl who takes our orders at the Chinese place is super happy, and her name is Wendy."

"I like this Wendy phase. And if you decide to revisit the emo days, please give me a heads-up. Like a note on the fridge?"

"You don't want me to Snapchat you the news?"

"Preferably not. But skywriter is acceptable." I nod to the screen. "What else do you have, Annie Leibovitz?"

She clicks to the next shot. It's a completely goofy selfie where she sticks out her tongue, tilts her head sideways, and makes her eyes bug out. "Oops. I wasn't supposed to show that to you," she mutters, covering the screen with her hand as she navigates away from the image.

"Why?" I ask curiously.

She mumbles, "It's for your Christmas present."

And my heart melts into a huge puddle. I wrap

an arm around her and squeeze her shoulder. "I won't tell Santa you're giving it to me. I love it."

"You do?" she asks, both hope and worry in her tone.

"Of course. It's amazing. In fact, I can't think of a thing I'd rather have." I mean it from the bottom of my heart. This is the perfect gift. Because she knew I'd love it. Because she did it for me. Because she's smiling, and being silly, and knowing I love her.

"Are you enjoying your photography class?" I ask as I take a drink of my honey-drenched tea. I need to keep my vocal cords well-lubed since I'm asking them to do more heavy lifting than usual.

She pushes her glasses higher on the bridge of her nose. "It's a lot of fun. You should take a photography class."

"You think so?"

She shrugs. "Or take whatever you like. If you could learn something just for fun, what would it be?"

I consider that for a minute, and the answer arrives as Chloe moves her mittens away from her hot chocolate.

"Knitting," I say with certainty. "I'd like to take my knitting to the next level."

"I love your mittens though," she says, holding up the red and gray pair I made for her last year.

"But I want to learn cool patterns and stuff. And I

want to make sassier hats. All I make are these standard ones." I tap my seashell-pink hat.

"Sassy Hats," she says, as if she's testing out the words together. "Sassy Hats by Ally."

"My next career."

"I'd buy a sassy hat from you, Aunt Ally."

I force my smile not to slip when she calls me that. Really, what do I expect? I'm not her mom. I'm her aunt, the sassy hatmaker.

She shuts down the computer and reaches for her hot chocolate, wrapping her hands around it as she takes a sip. A dash of whipped cream decorates her top lip.

"You have a mustache," I tell her as I take another drink of tea.

"Maybe I want to have one," she says in a silly voice.

"Maybe add a beard, then," I say, and then I tell myself it doesn't matter what she calls me. *This* matters. How she is with me. She's playful and sharp, and she's shared her work with me. That matters more than a name, more than a title.

She dips her finger in the mug, scoops off some whipped cream, and slashes some over her chin.

"No fair. No one told me we were making whipped cream beards today," a deep baritone booms.

I look up to see Miller joining us. His hazel eyes

sparkle with delight, and his smile makes my heart do a little kick.

My stomach decides to get in on the action, flipping and flopping as I linger on his square jawline, his lips, his lean, ropy body.

I grab my tea and take another drink, desperately needing something to do besides gawk at my best friend like I've only just noticed he's one of the most attractive men ever in the history of the universe.

"I better get two hot chocolates, then, if we're making beards," he says.

I rise and grab his arm. "No."

"What?"

"That night you had two, remember? After we went to see *Jumanji*? You made me promise to never let you drink that many again."

"That's true," Chloe chimes in. "I pinky-swore to hold you back."

"Ladies," he says with a sigh as he shakes his head, "I'm a lost cause. I had a half dozen with Campbell the other week. You can't save me. Save yourselves."

"Can I have another, then?" Chloe chimes in sweetly.

"Because Miller is a piggy?" I ask.

Chloe laughs. "Seems fair."

"Yes," I say, giving her permission.

Soon, he returns with the drinks, adding a dollop above his lips.

Grabbing her camera, Chloe snaps a picture of him. Then she takes one of me when Miller swipes some whipped cream under my nose. I laugh, then wipe it off as Chloe gives him the same tour of her pictures she gave me. He pays rapt attention, asks questions, and shares his thoughts.

And the whole time, I'm thinking about licking that dollop of whipped cream off his lips.

Later, after Chloe goes to bed, Miller and I spit-shine and polish our song at my kitchen counter while I start on a new hat with a pink skull-and-crossbones design for Sam.

"Are you ready to record tomorrow?"

"I am," I say, and that's the understatement of the year.

"Will you be wearing your wig?"

"I should, right?"

"If it's part of your persona, yeah. Are you going to keep up the whole Honey Lavender style?"

As my needles click, I swallow and ask nervously, "Do you like it?"

He looks me over and licks his lips. "Hell, yeah."

I want to ditch the yarn, yank on the wig, and

model it for him, then ask in a sexy, sultry tone if I turn him on.

But I can't give voice to those feelings, nor can I give in to them. I'm doing this with Miller for the chance to make a little extra to support Chloe and me. I'm not doing this to scratch an itch for thirty days.

Sex itches can be scratched with battery-operated friends.

I'll do what any brave heroine faced with a challenging task would do—badass her way through it with a sword, never giving in, never surrendering.

Before he leaves, we play a quick game of Bananagrams, unleashing our inner twelve-year-olds when he plays *titular* and I build *dongle* off his *L*. We decide that those two words are so quintessentially dirty-but-not that we might as well make the game a tie.

"I wish you a titular goodnight," he says with a wink as he heads to the door.

"May you have a wonderful dongle," I say, but I can't stop laughing, and I'm glad Bananagrams has rerouted my racing hormones.

Once he's gone, though, the silliness stops, and so does my laughter.

Instead, all night long I fight off images of him. His hazel eyes flickering with desire. His strong body, moving over me. His lips brushing mine.

The next day, those images intensify, so I take out my imaginary sword of resolve and slash them to tattered bits.

I head to the recording studio, prepared to do battle with my newfound and most inconvenient lust.

CHAPTER 15

Miller

As I sing to Ally, I tell myself I could just as well be singing with Campbell or Miles. "*Maybe, if you come back to me . . .*"

But hell, I wouldn't sing those words *to* my brothers. We'd sing them together to an audience of faceless thousands.

Only, Ally is my audience, and I'm hers, and I should not be thinking of what my audience would look like in my bed.

Stunning, and hovering on the edge of pleasure.

I part my lips to sing the next line. "*Maybe if you come hard with me.*"

I groan in frustration as I botch the line of a song I wrote a few months ago and tweaked on my piano the other day for the two of us. My hormones are having a fucking field day. Little evil imps.

Ally stops, gesturing *take five* to the engineer in the sound booth.

She closes the distance. "You're stiff."

Stiff. She doesn't know the half of it. Iron spikes have nothing on me. Because Honey Lavender is in the house, singing, dancing, shimmying, and raising my flagpole.

"You need to let go," she tells me, smoothing her hands over my shoulders, and even that's arousing.

Everything is with her today.

She's like a sultry torch singer. She might as well don a red satin dress and slink her way across a baby grand piano, singing Billie Holiday's "These Foolish Things."

And I'd be that guy in the smoky, dimly lit jazz club, wearing a dapper suit, unable to take my eyes off her as she seduces me with bedroom eyes and her bourbon voice.

Only, I can't be that guy. I can't let my best friend turn me into a full-blown horndog.

So instead, I'm a robot today.

Clunky and awkward and banging into everything.

I never ever had these problems when I sang with my brothers.

Obviously.

"I'm all good," I say, like I'm one cool cat. I roll my shoulders as if all I need is to slough off the day's worries.

"You've been tense all morning."

Singing with her is the cruelest torture, and it's killing me not to grab her and yank her against me during every verse.

"Sorry. Didn't sleep well last night," I lie. I slept like a baby. I had a jerk followed by eight full hours, just like the doctor ordered.

She tugs my hand, pulls me through the booth and out into the hall. Weirdly, it's more private here.

"Miller, you know what made us click the other day?"

I shrug, shoving a hand through my hair in frustration.

"You said it yourself. It was chemistry."

"Right. Sure. We sounded good together."

"And we looked good together," she says. "Don't forget that. We had that *je ne sais quoi.*"

"Fine. We had some *je ne sais quoi*. Where did it go?" I pretend to look around. "Is it down there?" I point to the end of the hall. "Is it hiding under the carpet?"

She sets her hand on my heart, and my breath hitches. "It's here. It's us. It's our friendship."

"It is?"

She nods, certainty in her eyes. "Yes. It gives us a freedom to be physical with each other. A hand on an arm, a naughty look."

That's from friendship? I thought it was from this bizarre new desire to fuck her, which I NEED TO IGNORE TILL THE END OF TIME.

"Is that so?"

"Yes. Because we know each other. Because we trust each other. We're like . . ." She stares at the ceiling as if hunting for the right analogy. "Like dance partners. Don't be afraid to dip me, or spin me, or bend me."

I let out a tight breath, and the tension starts to fade. She's telling me to be physical. She's telling me to give in. For the sake of the music. "You're saying we should be a little flirty?"

"Yes. I won't bite." She shimmies her hips like she's loosening up for an exercise class. "Let's have fun. Let's play with the words, let's get in character."

"You want me to pretend I want to get it on with my singing partner?"

She lifts an eyebrow playfully. "Kind of? We had a sort of sexy energy the other day. Let's try to recreate it."

She jerks her chin toward the studio door, the twinkle in her blue eyes saying, *C'mon, partner.*

"Let's do it," I say confidently.

She pushes on the door and heads back inside, her tight ass looking edible in those painted-on jeans. And hey, she's giving me permission to think of her this way. I return to the studio, letting my dirty thoughts come out to play.

* * *

She's inches away and her voice is thrumming through me, her energy filling my motherfucking head with thoughts, with wishes. I pour them right back into the lyrics, letting my newfound desire fuel my performance.

"*Maybe, if you come back to me . . . Maybe if there was a way,*" I sing to her.

"*Maybe if there was a way . . . you'd be mine,*" she belts out in that throaty, sexy new voice of hers.

"*Tell me again,*" I croon.

"*You'd be mine,*" she sings right back to me, flashing the sexiest smile I've ever seen. It turns me on wildly.

I let it turn me on.

She gives a little nibble on the corner of her lips, a shake of her hips.

I'm dead.

Just fucking dead with desire for her, and when the next line comes around about how I'd run to her, I go all in. I grab her waist, threading one hand around her hip, and pull her close, singing about looking into her eyes.

In hers, I see the same fire and heat that burns through me.

And just like that, I know we're in this together. We're performing. We finish the song, barely any space between us, and it's hot as hell.

She thrusts her arms into the air. "That was amazing. See? You let go and got into it. That's how I do my audiobooks. I tell myself I'm Princess Malindia, and I'm vanquishing all my enemies."

God, I want to vanquish her.

I want to conquer her in my bed, and on my kitchen counter, and in the shower . . .

We rehearse a few more songs, and when afternoon rolls around, Jackson arrives. He shoots some footage of us prepping, then we decide to tackle our original song one more time.

He joins us in the studio, but I pretend he doesn't exist. I sing to Ally, only she's not Ally. She's Honey, this brand-new woman, and I don't take my eyes off her.

She doesn't look away either. Those sapphire

eyes pin me the whole time, and when we hit the chorus, I'm on fire.

Flames lick my neck, and my blood heats, roaring to temperatures I've never experienced before. Call the fire department. When I sing the words about making her mine, I go bigger, yank her close, and I swear no one else is here. When we near the end, I let instinct take over. I thread my hand around her neck, and her breath catches as I sing the last words. I run my hand up into her fake blonde hair. She gasps, and I growl.

Everything goes quiet as the notes fade out.

Jackson clears his throat. "Want me to get a fire extinguisher?"

* * *

An hour later, Jackson waves like a madman from the booth, calling Ally and me over. He points wildly to his phone. "Dude. You have to see this. This is on fleek."

"Courtesy to speak English."

"It means on fire," Ally says.

Jackson stabs the screen. "I posted it to YouTube. It has sixteen hundred views in thirty minutes. Look at the comments."

Must leave work now to go jump my BF.

I just combusted.

OVARIES!!!!!!

That song is hot, but the way they look at each other is hotter.

Ally turns to me, wide-eyed. "Virtue Moir," she whispers, wonder in her voice.

"What's that?"

She fans her face with her hand then grabs my shoulder. "They think we're Virtue Moir."

"Courtesy to speak English."

Ally's words tumble out in a rush. "They're a Canadian ice-dancing couple from the recent Olympics. Audiences obsessed over them. They're crazy talented, and they're also beautiful and sexy, and he skated with her like he was in love with her."

I wrench back when she says those words.

She rolls her eyes and laughs, slugging my arm. "Don't worry. I know you're not in love with me. But he skated with her like that. It was gorgeous, and you couldn't look away." She raises her hand to her neck and drags her fingers along her skin. "He'd kiss her neck and run his hands down her arms," she says, and I can't look away from her hand. I want to travel where those fingers are visiting. I want my lips to map that path. "He'd lift her high above his head, and when he lowered her, he'd stare at her like he wanted to rip her clothes off."

I understand this man completely.

I want to know what Ally looks like under those jeans. What color panties she's wearing. If they're tiny and pink and covered with hearts. If they're wet. How she looks when I tug them off her.

"And that worked for them?" I rasp.

"Audiences went wild. They were the talk of the games."

She grabs her phone and does a quick search right here in the booth, showing me video after video, gif after gif of the skating duo. Holy fuck. She's right. They're so hot, they're turning *me* on, and I'm not into ice dancing.

But it's true—you can't take your eyes off them because he skates with her like it's foreplay. Like he wants to take her home and strip her. Hell, he skates like he wants to take her right there on the ice.

She's the same with him. She cups his cheek in a desperate sort of way, threads her hand in his hair, and her lips seem to beg his for a kiss.

"Um, two thousand views. And more comments," Jackson announces, thrusting his phone at us, scrolling over the comments on our video.

Aretheyoraren'tthey?

OMG, they're so pretty . . .

He is going to have her for dinner tonight.

I turn to Ally, blinking in surprise, wondering how they read my mind.

Use it.

I take her hand, lead her back to the studio, and launch right into "Need You Now" with her once more, since she secured the rights for us to sing this tune.

I play for the camera the whole time, singing to her, touching her shoulder, her hair, her hip. I go for broke at the end. After I finish my last line and the music carries us, I brush my lips to her neck. She shivers in my arms, a tremble that I swear moves through her whole body. I drag my lips lower down her neck till she lets out a soft gasp. It turns me on ferociously.

The tiniest gasp escapes her lips, a sound so soft, a noise so sensual, it sends a fresh wave of heat through my body.

I should stop, but I don't. I kiss the hollow of her throat. She trembles against my lips, and even though we're not alone, it feels entirely private—this kiss, her reaction, my desire. It feels like ours alone, whether the camera is rolling or not.

It makes me want to kiss her senseless.

But you always leave the audience wanting more. Slowly, I pull away, my lips already missing her skin.

Her eyes float closed for a moment as she sings the last words. When she opens them, I wonder if she's acting too.

Or if everything just got real.

CHAPTER 16

Ally

That two thousand views in an hour multiplied.

Exponentially.

What started as a let's-post-this-online experiment has steamrolled. I know the drill, since I've been here with Kirby. But it wasn't our first YouTube video that took off like proverbial wildfire. It was our seventeenth.

This time, the first one with Miller is a hot, sexy charm. And so's the second, when Jackson posts the next day with another song Miller wrote and tweaked for us.

Now, three days later, those two thousand views have avalanched into half a million views. The second video? It's riding the coattails at a hefty 350,000 views already.

The comments are endless, a river of *Whoa, is it hot in here*, *Mr. Hot Stuff and the sexy blonde*, and *Hashtag ZimmerHart*.

I can't complain, and neither will my bank account. The money is a trickle now, but as the views grow, so will the ad dollars, and every little bit helps when you have someone besides yourself to look out for. I shoot Miller a quick note while walking home on Saturday evening after picking up Vietnamese sandwiches for dinner with Chloe.

Ally: This is amazing! We need to keep this up!

Miller: I'm on the piano as we speak.

Miller: Well, I'm not literally *on* the piano. If I were a cat, I'd be *on* the piano. I'm not a cat.

Ally: Thank you for the clarification. I did wonder.

Miller: Technically, I was typing on the phone. But my ass is on the piano bench, and my fingers are on the keys. And I'm purring . . .

Ally: Meow. Keep going, pussycat! We have fans already! Eeek, fans!

After dinner, Chloe heads to the shower, and I read the comments on our videos once more, shaking my head in amazement. It really does seem the internet likes what Miller and I have going on—our music, our songs, but especially our chemistry.

So does Macy.

As I make a pot of tea, my phone pings with a text from her.

Macy: Damn, woman. Have you seen these videos? I think I'm pregnant from just watching you and Miller.

Ally: When you have your second baby, please name it Immaculate.

Macy: Oh, sorry. What did you say? I just jumped your brother. We're having twins.

Ally: La la la la. I CAN'T HEAR YOU.

Macy: Seriously, this is so hella hot I don't even know if there's a temperature that can record how incendiary it is. I can't stop watching you two. And I'm not alone. Your videos are burning up the charts.

Ally: It's crazy, isn't it? It was never like this with Kirby.

Macy: Well, let's hope not! But I need you to tell me the truth. Are you dying for Miller? When I watch those videos, all I can think is that you must have climbed him like a redwood tree when the cameras stopped rolling.

Ally: No trees were scaled, I assure you. We simply have stage chemistry.

Macy: I can literally hear you lying through the transom of text.

Ally: I swear, Macy! There's nothing happening.

Macy: Not a thing? Not even a little bitty flicker of a thing?

Ally: When we sing, we're performing. We both just go into character. That's all.

Macy: Bummer. I was hoping for one final salacious tale before I leave for Boston.

Ally: Fine. I'll give you one little nugget. I *might* have felt a flicker of a spark when I went ice skating with him last week, but I think it's normal to be attracted to someone you perform with. That's what happens when we're in the studio. But what's important is what to do with the attraction.

Macy: Act on it?

Ally: No. Channel it into the music. Acting on it would ruin our band and ruin our friendship.

Macy: All I'm saying is Kirby and I were friends, and now look at us. It can work. :)

Ally: Yes, but you and Kirby were on the same page. Miller's not, and I respect his wishes. It's best if we let our unusual chemistry fuel the music. Only the music.

Macy: I bet it winds up fueling your pants.

Macy is determined to make her point. She fires off a string of text-message gifs—Blanche from *The Golden Girls* spritzing water on her flushed skin,

James McAvoy fanning himself with a sheet of paper
. . .

Laughing at my friend's antics, I set the phone on the counter as an image of a cat basking in much-needed air-conditioning pops up on my screen.

While Chloe's hair dryer whirs from the bath-room, I squeeze honey into a mug, and consider Macy's efforts to break me down. She's not wrong. I would absolutely like to climb Miller. In fact, I'd like to ride him like a rodeo bull. *Yeehaw.* I'd saddle him up and reverse cowgirl him till the cows came home.

Have him tie me down with rope . . .

Wait, do I have a Western fetish?

No, that's not the case, because my brain serves up an image of Miller pinning my wrists in an eleva-tor, then on a bed, then in a town car.

Well, that's clear now. I don't have a Western thing. I have a Miller thing. As my belly swoops in a dirty roller-coaster ride, it's a thing my body wants me to act on.

But there are choices, and then there are *foolish* choices. They have the most foolish of consequences.

When Chloe clicks off the hair dryer, she pads into her room and calls out to me, "Can you braid my hair, Aunt Ally?"

"Of course." I shove away the dirty thoughts to focus on my girl.

I find her on her bed, brushing her hair, wearing

her doughnut pajamas. I take a drink of my hot tea, place the mug on her nightstand, and hop onto the bed beside her. She hands me a hair tie and I move behind her, sitting cross-legged as I gather chunks of her red hair. "What was your high and low today?"

She hums then answers, "High was when Hailey and I decided we should go bowling together over break, and maybe binge-watch a new show we like. I love bowling."

"Bowling rocks. I like this plan. And your low?"

Her shoulders sag a bit. "Low was talking to Uncle Kirby. He called me when you were picking up dinner."

"Why would that be a low, Monkey?"

She sighs. "Because I'm going to miss him and Aunt Macy when they move."

"Me too," I say wistfully, weaving another strand of her hair. "It'll be strange not to have them nearby."

"I know. But I'm glad you're not the one moving away."

Startled, I drop her hair and scoot forward so I can look her in the eyes. "Sweetie, I'd never move away from you."

Her lips are a tight line before she seems to force out a shaky question. "You wouldn't?"

My throat catches. "Monkey, you're stuck with me."

A little smile seems to sneak out. "Okay. Good."

I squeeze her shoulder, wanting her to feel reassured completely. "You're stuck with me for good."

She shrugs. "Well, Uncle Kirby *is* leaving." Her eleven-year-old logic must seem ironclad to her. Poor kid.

"Chloe," I say, fighting back the hitch in my voice. I need her to feel my strength. I need her to know deep in her gut I'll be here. Always. "It's not the same. I'm your guardian. I made a legal promise to the state, and I made a promise to my sister. It's an unbreakable vow. You know that, right?"

"I think so."

"Know so," I tell her firmly, as I look her in the eyes. "You're mine. That's an unbreakable promise too. It's my promise to you."

A little tear forms in the corner of her eye as she sniffles. "I don't want you to go."

I wrap my arms around her, trying to pour all my love for her into her little body. "I'm not going anywhere. And if I ever go somewhere, you're coming with me. You and me—we go together."

She pulls back and holds up her pinky. "Package deal?"

Laughing, I wrap my pinky around hers. "I swear."

"Well, now that we've pinky sworn," she says softly, then her shoulders rise and fall, as if she's letting the last of her tears escape, "can you go back to my hair?"

"Of course," I say, relinquishing my shrink role and returning to my hairdresser job. Tomorrow, I'll wear another hat, then another. Good thing I like hats.

As I finish her hair, she tells me how excited she is for tomorrow since we're heading to Campbell's in the early evening to decorate his Christmas tree. After I tie off the ends of her braid, I wrap my arms around my little monkey and give her a kiss on the forehead.

"Do you want to watch an episode of *Girls Rule*?"

"What's that?"

"It's this new show about a girl band in high school. I figured since you're a girl, and you're in a band, you might, I don't know, like it," she says, that deadpan Chloe back in full force.

"Sounds like my kind of show."

And it sort of is. It's cute and kitschy, but the girls can *hella* sing, as Chloe says.

When the episode ends, I say goodnight and return to the living room. After I review some pages from an upcoming book about the exploits of a hyper-sarcastic sixteen-year-old who hosts her own sports radio show, I grab my phone, perusing the texts from Macy once more.

Did we really look that hot?

I sink onto the couch, pop in my earbuds, and find one of the videos of Miller and me. I hit play. Seconds later, a tremble rushes through me as I watch Miller kiss my neck. A shudder runs roughshod over my skin as I study the look on my face on the screen. I slow down the video, pausing it.

Holy shit.

That *look*.

It's like rapture. Like bliss.

I close my eyes and recall that moment in the studio, how I felt with Miller's lips on my body.

I felt like a stranger in a strange new land, one I wanted to travel to again and again. I picture myself there, being kissed on my neck, my ear, and my lips. My skin heats from the inside out. My breath comes faster.

Awareness dawns on me like the sun rising. I could stay here in this land where Miller and I kiss and touch and lose ourselves in each other.

But it's too risky.

Too dangerous.

I snap open my eyes.

I didn't start a band with Miller to fall into his arms. There's a sleeping girl in the other room who needs me to always be here for her, to take care of her. The band is supposed to be part of that. It helps me provide for her, and the better Miller and I lure in fans, the more money we earn.

I allow myself one last peek at the video then hit end. Resolved, I grab Chloe's school bill and write a check for the next tuition installment.

* * *

The second the door to Campbell's spacious apartment snicks shut, I'm greeted by a chorus of "Hashtag ZimmerHart."

Guess that name won't die.

Mackenzie cups her hands around her mouth, calling out the title bestowed by the viral masses, while her good friend Roxy whistles in appreciation. Miles joins in, shouting, "The other half of Hot Stuff is here." From his spot on the couch, Miller seems to soak in the praise as he grins at me. That smile of his does funny things to my chest.

Things I can't entertain.

I try to make light of the comments, smiling as I yank off my mittens and take Chloe's hat, stuffing both in my purse. "We're just having fun."

"Sure looked like the kind of fun I'd like to have," Roxy says as she flicks a strand of her long red hair out from under her Mrs. Claus hat.

"It's crazy fun for me too. I've never captured anything on video like this," Jackson says as he rummages through a bowl of popcorn that Campbell's daughter made.

I do my best demure smile, since that comes easily to me. "See? It's fun for everyone." I gesture to the tree to deflect attention. "Let's tackle this bad boy."

* * *

But the talk of the new musical duo dominates even as we decorate Campbell's monster-size Christmas tree.

"You guys are going to be the next big thing," Mackenzie says, her brown eyes sparkling as she rifles through a storage box, snagging a horseshoe ornament. "When will we see you on stage?"

"First show is next week," I say, bouncing on my toes as I hang a fake candy cane from a low branch. "We booked a gig opening at a club in Soho."

Her smile radiates. "That's amazing. And you're just a little excited, I take it?"

Laughing, I adjust the candy cane around a string of lights. "However could you tell?"

"I knew the two of you would work out," Campbell says confidently, while hanging a mini stuffed-fox ornament in the middle of the tree.

"Of course it's working out. She has the voice of a sexy angel, plus she's better-looking than my brothers," Miller says with a wink as "Santa Claus Is Comin' to Town" blasts from the sound system.

Campbell claps him on the back. "Why play with your washed-up brothers when you can sing with a very lovely lady?"

Miles clears his throat dramatically, striding over to the tree with his son by his side. "Speak for yourself. I'm not washed up. Am I, Ben?"

Miles lifts his son to reach a high branch in the tree with a mini wooden caboose.

"No, Daddy. You took a shower this morning. I took a shower too. I decided I'm too old to take baths," Ben says, informing us of his big decision.

Mackenzie pinches her nose. "I don't care for baths either. It's like sitting in a pool of dirty water."

I snap my gaze to her, dropping my jaw. "You don't like baths? I love luxuriating in the tub when I have the rare chance."

She shakes her head adamantly. "I don't have a tub, and I don't miss it."

Roxy raises a glass of eggnog. "Hear! Hear! I have a tub, but I don't use it. I'm all shower, all the time."

"A woman who loves showers," Miles says in a raspy tone, wiggling his eyebrows at the leggy redhead.

I shift my gaze from him to her, and I swear he's picturing Roxy in the shower. The dirty pervert.

Sam's voice slices across the chorus. "Excuse me," she booms like a megaphone. "Anyone else think it's unacceptable that the adults are talking about baths in front of us? If you're under eighteen and mortally offended, raise your hand."

Jackson laughs and lifts his hand. Mackenzie's son, Kyle, shoots up his palm. Chloe raises hers too. Sam sweeps through the living room, scoops up her towheaded cousin, and makes the youngest kid in the room wiggle his fingers. "See? Ben agrees."

With him perched on her hip, she points accusingly at the lot of us. "All of you are hereby forbidden from discussing your bathing habits henceforth and forever and ever. Amen."

Ben giggles and Sam gives him a big smoochy kiss on his forehead.

"We're so sorry," Mackenzie and Campbell apologize in unison, complete with bows of supplication.

"You're forgiven," Sam says magnanimously.

"No more bath talk, Ally," Miller says to me in a low, flirty voice.

I press my hand to my chest, ever the innocent. "Hey! The bath talk was hardly my fault."

"I know," he says, his voice dipping into a low growl, "but now I know you're a mermaid."

My lips part, and heat splashes across my cheeks. He makes *mermaid* sound like the most decadent word in the English language.

"And are you a merman?" I ask quietly, as I stretch to adjust a trio of silver and purple ornaments on a high branch.

"I do like water," he says with a wink. "Let me help."

He slides in closer to me, his freshly showered scent flooding my nose. A flush climbs over me while he finds just the right branch for the ornaments, whispering in that rough voice again, "Also, I'm not opposed to baths with mermaids."

His eyes darken, shimmering with desire, the way they do when he sings with me. The way that's dangerous. I swear, I can feel a full-body tremble coming on, like a Mack truck barreling down the highway.

But it's best to avoid gasping, sighing, or panting in front of the whole crew, so I square my shoulders like I can fight off the desire that's picking up speed as the flush spreads down my chest.

My hormones are saved from a public show when the opening notes of "Frosty the Snowman" fill the room.

"I love Frosty," Ben shouts.

God, me too, since Frosty is taking my focus off my out-of-control libido.

Campbell dives into the first few lines, singing about two eyes made out of coal. Soon his golden tones are twined with those of his brothers, telling a tale of a snowman that comes to life.

The look on Miller's face is pure joy, and I'm keenly aware he can't ever resist the chance to knock out tunes with his former bandmates. *His favorite bandmates.*

My heart hurts a little, knowing he'll always prefer them.

But I can't compete in that department. I don't have the equipment or the DNA, so there's no point. I remind myself not to feel threatened by them, even mentally. Instead, I enjoy the special concert as the three former teen heartthrobs serenade their families with Christmas music.

When the tune ends, Mackenzie springs to her feet, clapping so loudly it must hurt her palms. "Encore! Encore!"

Miller looks to his brother, snaps his fingers, and says, "Do you recall . . .?"

And the trio rocks out to "Rudolph the Red-Nosed Reindeer" as the rest of us chime in with the chorus. They slide into "Have Yourself a Merry Little Christmas" next, and at the end of that song, Campbell walks over to the spacious leather couch, sets his hands onto Mackenzie's shoulders, and sings the final lines to her.

My heart melts into a puddle from the love they share—it's like it has its own life force. It fills the living room. They're so madly in love it makes my chest ache.

It makes me *want*.

I have to look away, but when I do, I find Miller

watching me, maybe even cataloging my reaction to Mackenzie and Campbell—the new lovers, the happy couple.

Our eyes connect, and the back of my neck grows hot. I need to resist him for so many reasons, but when he gazes at me like that, my resolve starts to burn off.

"How about Miller and Ally?" Mackenzie shouts, and I frown.

"How about Miller and Ally what?" I ask, a little defensively. Did she catch on to something?

"A song," Mackenzie adds with a smile, and I breathe a sigh of relief.

"Let's do it," Miller says, catching my gaze again. He licks his lips and shoots me a wolfish smile. That's a new one, and it makes me feel like he can read my mind, dirty thoughts and all. Have I become an open book?

Campbell slices a hand through the air. "Hey, now, this is a family Christmas party, folks. Kids are here, so we can't have Hot Stuff sing."

"Is that our new band name?" Miller asks.

Campbell scratches his jaw, then nods. "It's better than Other Uses for Ribbons."

"It's not a bad name," I admit.

Miller smiles. "I like Hot Stuff. Want to sing a tune, Ally?"

But before I can answer, Campbell interrupts. "No way. You guys are Not Safe For Work. Or kids."

I blush but laugh it off. "We'll be good."

"We'll be great," Miller says. He grabs my hand, and my stomach flips when he slides his fingers through mine. Glancing down at our joined hands, my mind frolics further on tawdrier shores, picturing his fingers tracing my skin, my breasts, my belly.

Shake it off, Ally.

"We can be safe for kids, right?" Miller says in his sweetest, good-boy voice.

Speak for yourself.

He launches into a rousing rendition of "Jingle Bells," and I've no choice but to follow him there.

Chastely.

But tell that to my libido. Even with the hand-holding, and the dashing through the snow, my pulse is spiking dangerously by the end of the song, and I still want my best friend to slide his arms around me again, find some mistletoe, and kiss me under it.

Inappropriately.

Senselessly.

For hours.

When the song finishes, I force myself to let go of his hand so I don't grab him and slam him against me in front of everyone. Swallowing roughly, I walk to the kitchen area, grab the bottle of white wine, and pour myself a glass.

I might die of thirst.

Mackenzie joins me. "The guys sound amazing together."

"They do. This is the first time you've heard them sing together in person, right?"

"Yes. Do they do this every year?"

"They can't seem to resist singing together. Old habits die hard."

"But you and Miller sound great too. Are you having a blast playing with him?"

I contemplate that question as I glance at the other half of Hot Stuff. Miller's floppy brown hair falls onto his forehead, and his toothpaste smile flashes as he builds a Lego train with Ben by the newly decorated tree. Yes, *blast* is precisely the word I'd use.

It feels a little like my heart's being blasted by something unexpected.

Something I can't have.

Yet something I desperately want.

A little later, Jackson takes off, saying goodnight to our crew. Then Chloe unleashes an epic yawn, a sign that it's time to go.

Once I'm away from Miller, I'll be able to reset my mind. I'll knit a new hat and focus all my energy on needles and yarn, rather than sex and kisses.

Needles and yarn, I repeat silently.

I grab my coat and plan to say goodbye to Miller, figuring he'll head home.

But he says he'll go with me.

I try to rein in my wild grin and the galloping in my heart.

"We can work on our next song when Chloe's in bed," he says, by way of explanation.

I hate how much my heart leaps at the thought.

And I love it too.

CHAPTER 17

Ally

In the cab, Chloe yawns majestically but still details her plans for Christmas Eve. "We're going to order Chinese food, go to church, and make cookies for Santa."

"Gingerbread, I hope," Miller says as the cab swings down Broadway, dodging past cars and buses.

"His favorite, of course." She lets loose another epic yawn as her eyes flutter. In a heartbeat, her head sinks onto Miller's shoulder.

"Don't forget carrots for the reindeer," he says softly, patting her hair.

"We never forget the reindeer."

Somewhere south of Twenty-Third, a faint snore rumbles from my girl.

I smile at Miller, who's become her pillow. He grins back, and as I regard the tableau they make, my heart expands like a water balloon. It's too big for my chest. I'll need a new place to store this organ soon.

But it's precarious too. It'll pop any second.

When we reach my block, a quiet stretch of Sixteenth between Seventh and Eighth Avenues, the taxi stops, and I swipe my credit card to pay. Once the transaction is complete, I turn around to find Miller has lifted Chloe out of the cab, and she's still sound asleep in his arms.

It is one of the sweetest things I've ever seen, and as I shut the door to the cab, I mentally record the image—him holding her on a cold and quiet Manhattan street, with a hint of snow in the sky. In this tender moment, something shifts inside me.

Something unnamed, but something swollen with potential, with hope. This brand-new thing rattles around, both scaring and thrilling me.

I want *that*.

Right there.

Him.

My heart glows as I flash back on the sweet and silly ways Miller has come to take care of Chloe.

Checking out her photos.

Helping her with projects.

Joining us for dinner.

It's too much, the flip, flip, flip of images—Miller supporting Chloe. Chloe laughing with Miller. The moments. The days. All the times it's been the three of us. Everything aches inside me with a terrifying new longing. I've resisted closeness and eschewed intimacy because most of the men I've dated didn't want my baggage.

Miller has embraced it.

As a friend, I remind myself. *He's a friend to you and to Chloe.*

Grabbing a mental broom, I sweep those images of him and her out of sight. If I don't, I won't be able to make it through the next few minutes without flinging myself at him.

"You can set her down. She'll wake up long enough to make it upstairs," I say softly.

"I've got her," he whispers, and that's my cue to zip into action.

I scurry to the front door, unlock it, and hold it wide open for him. Then I race to the elevator and hit the up button. The lift arrives instantly, and we step inside, Chloe still slumped on his shoulder, slumbering. When we reach the third floor, I scramble down the hall to open the door to my apartment.

Miraculously, she remains in the land of nod. He carries her to her room and gently lowers her to the bed. I take off her glasses, set them on her night-stand, and tug off her boots. I help her out of her coat, a feat I somehow manage without waking her up. She lets out a small, soft sigh as I pull up the covers and tuck them under her chin, topping them with a white blanket covered in a ladybug pattern. Lindsay bought it for her when she was five. It was a birthday present, and she cherished it.

Chloe flips to her side, and I press the softest kiss to her forehead. Miller brushes his hand over her shoulder, a tender gesture that hooks into me once more. We leave her room, and in the doorway, we cast our gazes to the sleeping child at the same time.

Before the moment swallows me whole, I pull the door shut, and it clicks closed. I'm relieved to put that part of the night behind me. Pretty sure I can only withstand one full-body melting per evening.

"Wine and song?" I ask, since it feels exactly like wine o'clock right now.

"We'll crack open a bottle and tackle our next tune."

I pour two glasses of white and join him on my plush purple sofa covered in silver pillows and a teal throw blanket. I reach for my notebook so we can start brainstorming a song.

But he has other matters on his mind. "She still believes in Santa?" he asks curiously, reaching for his phone and finding a playlist. He shows me a list of

Billie Holiday and Frank Sinatra tunes, and I give a thumbs-up. He turns the volume low, matching the dim lights in my apartment.

"She does," I say, answering the question as Billie croons faintly. "A lot of kids her age don't, but she still does, so we do the whole routine."

"Do you think it's because she's had a tough life? That she wants to believe in something?"

I shake my head. "No, that's not it."

"What is it, then?"

Kicking off my suede ankle boots, I tuck my feet under me. "Do you remember believing in Santa? How wonderful it felt?"

He nods, an easy grin. "It was magic."

"That's why. She likes believing and it's a link to Lindsay and a happy time. I don't think there's any reason to dispel the notion until she's ready."

He lifts his chin. "What do you believe in? Baths? Knitting? Heartwarming movies? How much fun you have with me?" He smiles, but it holds a hint of nerves, like he's keen for my yes, and worried he won't get it.

"Of course I believe in you." I lean back, sinking into the sea of pillows. He pats his thigh, a sign for me to put my feet up on him. For a nanosecond, I consider the risk. But we've been there, done that. I can handle my feet on his thighs. I oblige, untangling them from under me and dropping them on his legs.

Miller tugs on my right sock, yanking it off my foot.

"You're stripping me," I tease as I take a drink, enjoying the wine and how easily we've slid back into familiar, friendly territory. Even the naughty flirting can't take us out of where we best belong.

"I want to check out your feet, woman."

I laugh as he tugs off the other sock. "Why on earth do you want to see my feet?"

"I'm not afraid of feet."

"You're an amazing man. So fearless."

"Watch it, or I might nibble on your toes."

I hold up a finger. "That, I believe in. Your ability to resist my toes."

"I wouldn't count on that." He tugs my foot toward his mouth, baring his teeth as if to bite my big toe. I wriggle away, and he laughs, letting my foot sink to his lap. He switches gears, digging his thumbs into my foot, rubbing. Instantly, I moan in pleasure.

"I believe in foot rubs. And I believe in your friendship," I say, because I want him to know no matter how much we flirt, I'll stay on this side of the divide, since that's what he wants.

And what I need.

He smiles as he kneads deeper into the arch of my foot. "What else do you believe in?"

I swirl the wine in the glass and take another

gulp. "I believe in good wine. I believe in tea with honey."

"I'll drink to that too." He grabs his glass and swallows, then returns to my feet.

I gaze at the window and the sky beyond, where a faint orange glow hints at snow. "I believe that when it snows in New York, wondrous things can happen that wouldn't ordinarily occur."

"Because of snow?"

"Definitely. Snow makes you believe that everything can be beautiful and perfect even for just a sliver of time. You look outside, and it feels calm and peaceful in this most crazy city."

He tilts his head as if considering that. "True. We know it won't be that way in the morning. Everything will change, and slush and dirt and honking trucks will take over once again."

"But at two in the morning, it's lovely."

His gaze strays to his phone, as if he's checking the time—12:09 lights up the screen. "It's not two yet." He digs harder into my feet, his eyes returning to mine. "But I'd like it to be."

As he looks at me, tingles slide down my body. I'd like it to be two in the morning. Two seems like the perfect time—the *only* time—for what I want. For a stolen hour with this man, for a moment I might regret but I'll take the chance on anyway because of how he makes me feel.

Like I'm floating.

Like I can do anything.

Like nothing would ever hurt if we crossed the line.

I spend so much of my time striving toward goals, planning for the future. What if I let go for one night? Maybe just once?

My breath catches, but somehow I find the words to keep the night unfolding. "What about you? What do you believe in?" I poke his stomach with my toe.

His hard stomach.

Whoa. Miller has firm abs. "Nice washboard. Been hiding these from me?" I press harder against his stomach.

He grabs my foot and drags my toes over the fabric of the Henley covering his abs. "I'm not hiding them anymore," he says.

I'm not a foot fetishist, and I don't think he is either, but I want to thank the good Lord for making toes, since Miller's using mine to let me cop a feel of his belly.

"I need to add your stomach to my list of beliefs. I definitely believe in your abs now. I've seen the light."

He laughs, tipping his head back, and I sneak a peek at the stubble on his jaw, at his alluring eleven o'clock shadow. *That stubble.* I want to feel it sliding against my cheek. I want to know its sandpaper scratch.

He looks down at my feet. "I believe that green toenail polish is adorable and sexy. I also believe that you have strangely beautiful feet."

"You do have a foot fetish," I whisper in surprise.

"I don't. I don't know why your feet are beautiful all of a sudden. They just are." But he's not looking at my feet. He's staring at my face, and my cheeks flush, hot from his gaze.

Have I had too much to drink? I feel tipsy, but I've barely touched a drop.

"What else do you believe in?" I ask, because I don't want to stop. I want us to touch in these little ways, to talk, and to tango mercilessly closer to a risky truth.

"My brothers. Hot chocolate. The good in young people like Jackson and Chloe." Answers pour out of him like water, his tone shifting to serious. "I believe in music too. I believe it's the one universal language in the world, and that songs can connect people. When I play and sing, I feel that connection with others. Like you."

"I believe in that too," I say, my voice feathery.

He drags a fingertip over the top of my foot, and I nearly cry out in pleasure. How is it possible to be ignited from a finger across my instep?

"I think people are happier when they listen to

music. Maybe they love more deeply, or kiss more fervently, or maybe they take someone to bed. I think music helps people to love. I feel like that's my small contribution to the world," he adds, and his expression is etched with a new vulnerability.

My heart slams against my rib cage. I love that he feels that way about what he creates.

"I'm happier when I'm listening to music," I whisper, as Frank Sinatra's voice fills my head, and Miller moves his hands up my ankle.

"I believe in Skittles too," he continues, darting back to his playful side again, and I release some of the tightness in my hands. "And ice skating and Donkey Kong. And I definitely believe in these calf muscles you have." He squeezes my calf, and I wriggle because it tickles. "Where have you been hiding these insane calf muscles?"

"Same place you hid your abs?"

He smiles as he rubs, and I'm right back in this brave new land of lust. I fight like hell to remember why Miller and I are a risk—but after midnight, desire is stronger than reason.

"You feel good like this," he says as he rubs.

I can hear my pulse hammer; I can feel every heavy and tender beat of my heart. I swallow, and my throat is dry. I'm thirsty, so thirsty for a kiss.

He squeezes my leg, like he's trying to get my attention. His eyes are etched with contrition. "I believe I'm a fool for not realizing we could sing so well together sooner, and I want to sing with you again. I want to make more music with you," he says, and it sounds like a desperate plea.

"Don't stop, then," I say, and I'm not only answering him. I'm telling him what I want.

"I believe, too, that sometimes lines get blurred," he says as his hands slide up my leg to my knee.

Movement at the window catches my eye. My pitch rises as I point. "Miller. It's snowing."

That's all it takes. He kneels forward, brushes my hair from my face, and brings his lips to mine. "Let's pretend it's two in the morning," he whispers against my mouth.

His lips sweep over mine, and the world blurs deliciously. As he kisses me, my body turns to honey. I sink into the dizzying sensation of our lips connecting, and I fall into this moment, so wonderful and lush, as his mouth explores mine. He nibbles on the corner of my lips, then kisses more deeply.

Our tongues skate together, and I pretend this isn't risky. I slide my hands up into his hair, threading my fingers through soft locks I've longed to touch without ever realizing.

Any question as to whether he feels the same escapes into the ether as I tug him closer. He presses his body to mine, his erection hard and heavy against me.

He's wildly aroused.

That's all I need to know.

I part my legs, wrapping my thighs around his hips, tugging him closer. I need the full press of him against me. I need his tongue, his lips, and his hard length. I want all of him with every cell in my body, and I kiss him that way, telling him with my lips that I don't want to hold back.

We're quiet though, perhaps both keenly aware of the sleeping child, but in the silence, we kiss like desperate creatures. Wordlessly, mostly soundlessly, we get to know each other's lips like we're giving ourselves something we were denied six years ago. Like this kiss, so long in the making, is the only thing we can think of doing tonight.

We kiss as if the night won't end, and as if choices don't have consequences. There's only the reward of sparks flying across skin, of blood heating, and of skin sizzling.

I rock my hips against him, desperately seeking more of Miller. His breath tastes like chardonnay and hunger, like he's been wanting me with a madness. A madness that's lasted for six years.

But I can't and won't forget that Chloe's in the other room. I break the kiss and peek over the couch. Her door remains closed.

"We'll hear her if she gets up," he whispers.

"I know. But we can't get naked with her here. Even in my room."

"I know," he says with a wicked grin. "But I love that you thought of that."

I cup his cheeks. "All I want is to be naked and under you," I say, and now I truly feel like I'm floating, like I'm falling. Because I'm not holding this in any longer. He groans, a sound so sexy I wriggle to get even closer.

He sucks on my jaw, whispering, "I want you so fucking much. But what are we doing?"

That's the question. I don't have the answer, and I'm not sure I can handle all that I want. I don't think he can either, so I choose a half-truth. "Maybe we need to get this out of our system?"

"You think so?"

I nod, giving us permission. Judging from the heavy weight of his cock against my thigh, Miller needs the very same things I need.

Friction.

Connection.

Most of all, a seal of approval that *this*—whatever it is—won't ruin *us*.

"But no sex. We're not having sex tonight."

He nods quickly. "We'll just scratch the itch."

"A sex-less scratch," I add, and he laughs.

"And tonight—it won't change anything?" he asks, like an attorney leading the witness.

"It won't change a thing," I whisper, wishing, hoping that's true. Choosing to believe it for now.

"After this, we'll go back to how we were. Friends."

"Yes," I reply. "Besides, everyone thinks we're doing it already. Why should they be the only ones who enjoy our chemistry?"

He laughs. "I think we ought to benefit too." He dips his face to my neck. "What do *you* think, Ally?" He drags his lips up to my ear, sucking on my earlobe.

I bite back a moan. "I think . . ."

He nibbles, and I can't form sentences. "You think . . .?" he supplies, waiting for me to fill in the Mad Libs of lust.

I rock my hips against his hard-on, so thick in his jeans. God, I want to feel him inside me, sliding that hard cock into my wetness. "I think . . ."

I can't get words out with him so aroused, with me so desperate. He licks the shell of my ear and my vision blurs. Heat pools between my legs, and I arch against him, eager and hungry.

"I want you," I blurt out.

"I think the same thing," he growls, his voice dirtier than I've ever heard it before.

I grab his ass, grinding up against him as he kisses my neck, sucks on my jaw. "Love that, baby. Do that again," he whispers.

"What part?"

"The way you rub your sweet little body against my cock." His dirty words send shivers of lust across my skin.

I work my hips up against him. He rewards me with a low groan in my ear. "Yeah, that reminds me of how you are in the studio."

I thrust up again. "How am I in the studio?"

"Hot," he whispers as his lips roam my neck. "Bothered," he says, dusting them over my mouth. "And turned all the way on."

I let out a small moan I can't hold in. "I am. I am that way."

"I know, and I love it. I love that the music turns you on. Makes you hot. Makes you wet."

You turn me on, I'm dying to say, but I let him think it's the music. It feels safer that way. "The music gets me so revved up. You too?"

Nodding, he swirls his hips, and then slams against me, and I swear, God, I swear, Miller dry-humping me is better than any sex I've ever had. "Fuck, baby. You're getting me going."

"Me too," I whimper.

Tension climbs my legs, swirls in my belly. I tingle everywhere. I'm drowning in a sea of wild, erotic sensations as my best friend fucks me with his clothes on.

God bless snow.

God bless music.

God bless wild abandon.

I feel it with him, the crazy rush of sensations, the heavy throb of desire. Digging my fingers into his clothed flesh, I bring him as close as I can. I need all the friction to tip me over the edge.

I'm dying for it. I'm chasing it. I rock harder, faster. Senselessly.

"Yes, baby. Let go. Just fucking let go for me. Want you to come. Need you to come," he urges in my ear, and I gasp, bite my lip, and let go, sparks and electricity flaring everywhere as I reach the crest.

I grab his face as my orgasm escalates. I need his lips to cover up my moans. I kiss him urgently, hiding my cries of pleasure.

When my orgasm ebbs, he's gritting his teeth, breathing out hard. "Just. Trying. Not. To. Explode."

I laugh. "I can take care of that for you." I open my mouth wide, letting him know what I'd like to do with him.

He growls, as he drags a finger over my bottom lip. "Do not tempt me. We definitely can't do that. But I want that so badly that now I'm going to think of my brothers."

I blink in confusion. "Wha?"

He pushes up from me, waving a hand in front of his crotch. "Instant boner eraser."

I crack up. "Brothers are good for that. By the way, we never worked on our next song."

He shrugs. "Win some, lose some. We'll work on it tomorrow. Our fans are eager for more of our . . . *Hot Stuff*." He gives me a wink. "That was pretty hot."

"It was," I say, and then, because we're playing with fire, I add, "Our music gets me in the mood for sure."

"It'll be our little secret that we're turned on by our tunes."

That's what this will be. A secret we gave in to one snowy December night, because we believed in wine, and Sinatra, and the mad lure of quiet, calm New York to make us feel like the world had winked off.

But a little later, I'm curled up in Miller's arms on the couch, and he's cuddling me, and this doesn't feel like giving in to a secret. This feels like giving in to the years.

That's the problem.

The big problem.

CHAPTER 18

Miller

"You're a good pillow," she murmurs, as she snuggles into the crook of my arm.

"Use me, then," I tell her, but she needs no invitation. She's already there. Her eyes are falling closed, her breath turning steady and slow.

I sigh happily—too happily for my own good, as I stare at the window while white flakes drift down. Ally was right about falling snow. It's a spell that lets you believe a moment won't end. That tricks you into thinking it can last all night long.

I don't want this moment to end. I want it to unspool into tomorrow and the next day too. Now, after midnight, the soft white flakes hypnotize me, convincing me that this *thing* could work.

This wonderful, fantastic, dangerous thing.

Her and me, wrapped up in each other's arms, like the sun won't rise in the morning and shine a light on all the ways we could crack.

But it will, and we will.

Because I can count. I can add up the numbers and conclude I'm not a guy who knows how to make a relationship work. Yes, I've had girlfriends, and yes, I'm absolutely a serial monogamist. But I'm not the type who goes the distance. I don't know how. Maybe because I've never been with someone who makes me want to try, and Ally can't be my test case. The risks are too great. I can already feel how much it would hurt to try and fail.

There's more at play.

There's Jackson. I can't screw up his chance for a scholarship by getting involved with my bandmate then—inevitably—messing things up with her, imploding the project and leaving him with no documentary. Then there's Chloe, and Ally's wishes for her.

I tear my gaze away from the snow and bring it back to the woman cuddled against me, her soft brown hair with its pretty lavender strands resting against her cheek.

I should go, leave this night behind us. Close the

book on this brief tryst like we planned to. But the thought of leaving is like a serrated knife in my gut. I don't want to lose this connection.

Maybe I'll stay a little longer.

I tug her closer and run my nose along her neck, inhaling her coconut scent. Thief that I am, I steal a midnight kiss, brushing my lips over her soft skin.

Sometimes, something hits you all at once. Something that's been in front of you all along slams into you hard. I'd be a fool if I said this feeling was unexpected. I'd be a liar if I claimed I never thought this would happen.

The truth is, I was wildly attracted to Ally the night we met. Poised to ask her out, I was shot down with her "do you want to be friends" comment. I'd been ready, so damn ready to ask for more. After only a few hours of talking to her at the arcade that evening, I knew I didn't want to take her home for only one night. I wanted to romance her with dinners, with bowling, with more arcade games, and with walks in the park.

It wasn't insta-love. But it was insta-like.

She was the kind of woman I imagined could break the spell of my bachelor ways. She dropped the hammer on that quickly, crushing the possibility.

So, friends it was, and I never imagined our connection would turn this deep, this tangled up, like those skeins of yarn in her knitting bag. Somehow, six years later, we've become so thoroughly wrapped up in each other's lives that I can't imagine how we'd separate. She's one of the longest relationships I've ever had. That's the issue. I don't want to stare down a time when there's no Ally in my life.

But I don't want to stop touching her either.

I press my lips to her neck, imagining all the other ways I can kiss her. All the places on her body I can explore with my lips. The back of her thighs, her tight nipples, the top of her ass.

Between her legs when she's hot and wet and hungry for me.

Like she was tonight. My God, I bet she'd have tasted like heaven on my tongue.

A moan escapes my lips as I brush her hair off her cheek and kiss the shell of her ear, fantasizing about kissing her all the fuck over.

Murmuring, she turns to me, maybe still asleep, but maybe awake enough. Her lips find mine, and she brushes hers against me, whispering, "I was dreaming of kissing you."

Whatever resolve I have—and it's debatable whether that's any at all—melts like the snow on a New York sidewalk. I kiss her, and it doesn't end. It's a long, lingering kiss, the kind that turns into yet another soft, deep, sensual one, then another. The kind that is scarily romantic but also hints of dirtier desires.

Her hands slide down my shirt, then slip under the fabric.

"Your belly is so sexy, I want to lick it," she whispers, and I wish I could give in to everything. All my nerve endings spark and sizzle at the prospect of her lips, her tongue, traveling over me.

"It's still the middle of the night," I murmur.

"Let's make the most of it."

I reach for her hand, sliding it up, over, and around my stomach. Letting myself savor the intoxicating exploration of her traveling across my body.

"Mmm," she murmurs as her fingers dip lower. "I believe in this too. Your cock."

I. Die.

Her nimble hands slide over the front of my jeans, cupping my erection. I grit my teeth because it feels too fucking good. So good, in fact, that I should push her away, but I don't.

Instead, I let her pop open the button to my jeans and slide her palm inside my briefs. I groan as quietly as I can as she touches my dick for the first time. Then, pleasure spirals as she wraps that soft hand around my shaft.

Nice and tight.

She grips me, and I see stars. I see planets. I witness supernovas.

Her blue eyes spark with such naughtiness that I let her stroke me once, twice, three times. The way she fists me makes my bones vibrate with something wild and hungry. I'm nothing but frayed electrical wires, sizzling, crackling.

"A little tighter," I urge, and she grasps harder, strokes me faster.

The air evacuates my lungs in a hot rush as she reaches the tip. I let loose a gravelly groan as she slides back to the base. Hard, rough tugs.

A few more strokes, a couple pumps, and I could come.

That won't do at all.

The image alone makes me find the will to remove her hand from my boxers. "Don't think for a second I don't want you to jack me off right now," I tell her, and it's a wonder I don't whimper from the loss of contact. It pains me—my dick throbs and practically screams obscenities at me for not letting her finish the job.

She smiles. "Don't worry. Your dick does good work communicating."

I laugh as I tuck myself back into my jeans and do them up. "Yeah, he's skilled in the fine art form of *hard* gestures."

She laughs too. "I think I have a good sense of what he's trying to say."

"Let me just kiss you for a while."

Not that kissing her is any less enticing. In fact, maybe it's more so. It goes to my head. It fries my brain. It makes me think crazy, wild, romantic thoughts.

Dangerous ones.

But what happens in Vegas has to stay in Vegas. What happens after midnight stays in the dark. When morning comes, we have to return to Ally and Miller, friends, bandmates, and no more.

It's still nighttime though, so I savor this kiss, this sweet devouring of her lips, her tongue, her mouth. "One more time."

One more time turns into another minute, then five, then ten, until I yank her up from the couch, carry her to her bedroom, and settle her into her bed, planting my palms on either side of her. "If I stay, I will do unholy things to your body."

She nibbles on her bottom lip. "Someday I'd like to know what those blasphemous things are."

Someday.

That word makes my chest ache. I'd like that someday too.

But it can't happen.

"We'll talk tomorrow, okay?"

"Of course we will."

Her certainty makes me grin. I bend down, plant one more kiss on her forehead. She smiles and sighs contentedly. "Goodnight, Miller."

"Goodnight . . . hot stuff." I head to the bathroom, wash my hands, and brush my teeth, since I have a toothbrush here. When I leave the room, I nearly jump out of my skin.

"Hey," I say nervously to a sleep-rumpled Chloe, who rubs her eyes as she stands outside the bathroom door.

"Hi, Miller."

"I'm just leaving," I say quickly, maybe more defensively than necessary. I don't know what she's thinking, but I hope it's G-rated.

"You can stay if you want. The couch is comfy."

"I should probably go."

"Do you want to hear something funny?" she says in a whisper, motioning to me.

"Sure, sweetie. Tell me something funny."

Her voice is a sketch in the night. "Ally thinks I still believe in Santa Claus."

My eyes widen. "Are you serious?"

She nods, a clever grin on her face. "I know there's no such thing as Santa, but I like believing in it. And I like letting her think I do." She brings her finger to her lips. "Don't tell her."

I shake my head. "It's our secret," I say to this sweet kid who melts my heart, just like the woman in the other room does.

That's the problem. That's the big fucking problem. I care for them both too much.

I ruffle her hair, then I get the hell out of there.

CHAPTER 19

Miller

Miller: Hey, hot stuff. Told you I'm not the kind of guy who dry-humps and doesn't text by six a.m.

Ally: I'm not sure you specifically did, but hey, that's clearly another point in your favor.

Miller: Hooray for points. Ready for a busy day at prom?

Ally: You remembered what I'm reading today. :)

Miller: Does that surprise you?

Ally: It shouldn't. You always remember. I guess I haven't stopped liking it.

Miller: Keep liking it. It'll keep happening. As for me, I'm all about the songwriting today.

Ally: Someone distracted you from songwriting last night. :)

Miller: Someone definitely distracted me, and I regret nothing.

But no regrets doesn't mean we have a free pass to mess around again. Today, I vow as I turn on the shower, I will resist the irresistible. A little later though, because I need to take care of this morning situation first. It's the same situation I faced last night when I returned home from Ally's place.

The solution isn't nearly as satisfying as the one she teased me with when I left. But the image of her mouth on me will do just fine.

Oh yes, that's way more than fine.

That's one of the ways showers are indeed much better than baths.

* * *

The moment of truth has arrived. With a deadly

serious expression, I plunk the first Dixie cup on the counter.

Beverly rubs her palms together. "Honestly, I didn't think you'd come back."

I scoff incredulously. "Oh, ye of little faith."

She rolls her eyes. "I knew you'd come back for the birth certificate. But I figured you'd forget all about the great test."

I fix her with a don't-ever-doubt-me stare. "There is nothing more important to me in this moment than testing the veracity of this candy's flavor." I take a deep breath. "Are you ready?"

She nods solemnly, brushing a few loose strands of hair back into her bun. "I am."

I stare intently. "There's no turning back, Beverly. Once you know, you can't *unknow* this."

She nods resolutely, like a soldier.

I line up four Dixie cups on the counter, showing her the contents of each one. Each cup contains a different color of candy—I doled it out in the hall before I came in. I move them around, Three-card Monte–style, mixing up the locations. Each one is marked on the bottom with the candy's color.

I slide the first cup to her in the taste test. She closes her eyes, fishes for the red candy, and pops it in her mouth. She chews thoughtfully. "It definitely tastes like cherry."

She works her way down the line, pronouncing grape, lime, and orange.

When she opens her eyes, I thrust my hands in the air in victory. "She shoots—she scores!"

Her eyes widen, and she smiles gleefully. "I got them all right?"

I tap out a beat on the counter. "You sure did, Beverly. You are a one hundred percent certified Skittle aficionado with taste buds like Giada De Laurentiis," I say, then show her the marks on the bottom of each cup. "You, Beverly, have dispelled the notion of a Skittles Matrix." I reach into the bag again and hand her a huge, unopened packet of Skittles. "Your reward."

She clutches the bag to her chest like it's a precious object, a teddy bear from her childhood returned safely. "Thank you. You certainly made my job a lot more fun. And I do appreciate it because this is the first job I've stayed in for a long time."

I tilt my head to the side, my curiosity stoked. "What do you mean?"

"You name it, I've done it. I was a short-order cook. I was a retail clerk. I've worked in an auto parts store and as a receptionist at a nail salon. Then I found this job. I've kept it for five years and counting. That's the longest."

"What do you attribute the longevity to?"

"Honestly," she says, lowering her voice to a whisper, even though no one's nearby since it's still lunch break, "the benefits. This job has really good benefits." She spins around in her chair, grabs an envelope, and hands it to me. "Plus, every now and then you meet somebody who makes your day interesting."

I flick open the envelope and verify that it's Jackson's birth certificate inside. "Thank you. I appreciate you doing this so quickly."

She shakes her head. "Sweetheart, I have you to thank. You made my day. In fact, you made *two* days. I guess you're one of the benefits now too, and so are these Skittles." She opens the bag and shakes a few into my palm.

I pop a red one in my mouth, savoring the cherry flavor. As I leave, I linger on that word, letting myself think about benefits.

All kinds of benefits.

Everything snaps into place, thanks to the power of red Skittles.

CHAPTER 20

Ally

I'm walking on sunshine today. I'm shiny and new. Forget these young adult novels that pay my bills. Someone ought to hire me today to model skincare.

I'm positively glowing as I read a toe-curlingly, heart-meltingly delicious first kiss at a prom scene for my sports-radio heroine. "As the pop music plays, and the lights flicker across the dance floor, Taylor sweeps his thumb across my cheek and brushes his lips to mine. He's soft and gentle, but full of longing too. I soar to the sky from a kiss at prom."

I exhale, stretch my arms, and tell Kristy I'm going to take five.

She pokes her head into my side of the booth,

holding up a hand to high five. "You are on fire today, girl." I smack her palm. "Can I have some of what you're having? I want that flow when I'm editing."

"It's one of those lucky days." I smile, as if I've got a secret, only I don't even know what that secret is. Except maybe it's that orgasms make you feel better about everything.

Or maybe it's that friendship and fooling around *can* coexist. Miller and I danced so seamlessly back onto familiar ground this morning, and I'm pretty damn ecstatic about that too. Who said a little nookie would ruin a friendship? Not this girl. We are all good. We slid back to our roles like the path was lubed.

Though that might not be the best word to use.

Because now I'm thinking below the belt again. Truth be told, I've kind of been thinking with my lady parts all day long. As I slick on some lip gloss in the restroom, checking out my reflection, those parts are thinking of Miller.

What if we had one more time? One more night? To truly get him out of my system?

I close the tube of gloss, leave the restroom, and nearly bump into our receptionist outside the door.

"Hi, Ally. You have a little gift, it looks like," she says with a conspiratorial smile and a curious glint in her eyes.

Frowning, I check out the padded envelope she

hands me, but there's no return address—only the words *From M*.

"Thanks, Meg. I appreciate you bringing this to me," I say, then spin around since I don't want to open this with an audience.

Anything from "M" has to be personal. Walking down the hallway, I reach inside and tug out a clear plastic bag filled with red Skittles and wrapped with a red polka-dot ribbon.

A shiver rushes through me as I snag the card tucked under the bow.

Red Skittles are my favorite. They taste like cherries. That gave me an idea. Call me.
M

I stop near the stairwell door and hit Miller's name in my contacts. He answers immediately.

"Tell me more about this idea," I say, setting my hand on my belly.

"Remember at the ice skating rink when you said people struck deals and arrangements?"

I remember every detail of that day—when I felt the spark and sizzle for him. "Yes. Why are you asking?"

"I did a little research, and I learned that one of those arrangements is a friends-with-benefits deal."

My jaw comes unhinged, clanging to the floor. He's asking me for *this*? "You want a deal?" I sputter.

"I enjoyed last night, and I thought you did too." He hums a worried note. "Shit, Ally. Did I fuck up by asking this?"

I answer at the speed of light. "No. I just want to be sure I understand what you're asking."

And confirm it's the thing I'm fantasizing about.

He breathes, sounding relieved. "Good. Because what I'm saying is this—what if we could keep the friendship and also enjoy some delicious red Skittles?"

"Courtesy to speak English." I need to know I'm not interpreting him through my own wishes. My face is hot. My bones are humming, and I'm *this* close to running a hand down my breasts because I *need* touch.

He takes a beat. "I want you naked. I want you naked and under me. Naked and over me. Naked and coming. Again and again."

There isn't a thermometer on earth that goes high enough to record my temperature. It's shot beyond the stratosphere. "That's English," I manage to say.

"What do you think?"

I think I'm an electric line and I could power a

whole city. "Yes," I blurt out, because I want that kind of benefit. "I say yes."

"Can I see you later?"

I can't even process what I'm doing in the next ten minutes. "I'll text you when I'm done."

I return to the booth, floating on a cloud of climactic possibilities. Sliding on my headphones, I open the book file on my iPad. I clear my throat, ready to tackle the next scene, when my phone buzzes. I need to turn it to silent.

But I catch a glimpse of the message on the screen.

One word.

Ribbon.

I slide it open to read.

Miller: One of the benefits is that I'm going to tie you up with that red ribbon, and I'm going to kiss you everywhere, run my tongue down your breasts, spread your legs, and devour you till you come on my lips. And then I will fuck you like you wanted me to last night. Till you're mindless with pleasure.

I stare, slack-jawed at the screen. Flirting is one thing —dirty texting is entirely another, and it's ridiculously arousing. I wriggle in the chair, wishing I could race out of here *this second*.

Instead, I close my eyes, take a breath, and will away the images, so my young adult book doesn't sound like the sixteen-year-old heroine walked into the NC-17 version of prom.

Though that's where I want to go tonight.

And I want to enjoy every single benefit.

CHAPTER 21

Miller

To say I'm eager would be an understatement. What I am is fired up.

It's not only because I'm going to learn if Ally tastes like cherries, or like honey, or like the woman I've wanted to touch for a long time now. Hell, maybe it's all three, and I'll take a triple latte of Ally, thank you very much.

It's also because I have an idea for a song.

After I talk to Ally, I meet up with Jackson in the lobby of my building and hand off the birth certificate.

"Dude, you are the man," he tells me.

"How's Grandpa?"

He taps his chest. "Ticker works fine, and blood pressure is normal. He's doing well."

"You are the man for taking him to his appointment." I point at him. "Also, I know you're going to nab that scholarship, and your documentary is going to be awesome."

"If you and Honey keep breaking out the hits, it sure will be." Jackson tilts his head. "Speaking of . . . any more songs up your sleeve?"

"Actually, I do have a particularly good idea for one." I tap my skull. "And that means I need to work on it right now while my brain is the Lincoln Center Fountain of ideas."

Jackson's dark eyes sparkle, and he beams. "A brand-new one. Can I record you putting it together?"

"It's going to be raw. I haven't even written anything down yet. You'll be watching the sausage get made, my friend. You cool with that?"

He pumps a fist. "It's sausage time." He shakes his head like a dog then looks at me sheepishly. "You need to pretend I never said that."

I laugh as we head to the elevator. "It's already been erased from the gray matter."

Once we're upstairs in my place, he's quiet, the unassuming documentarian, as I grab a notebook, pace around my pool table, and jot down some ideas about chemistry, connection, and where it can take you.

I swear I can taste the song like it's sugar, like it's a swirl of sweetness on my tongue. The notes are playing in my head.

I head straight to my piano and tap out some notes and a few melodies.

That's not quite right. But what if I tried *this*?

I experiment with a different chord progression. Soon, I lose track of Jackson, and the time, and the camera, and everything but the music. My fingers fly across the keys, and I play with words and lyrics.

It's rough. It's raw. It's nowhere near a finished song. But it's coming together.

"Coming Together."

I like the sound of that, so I stop, scratch the words down as a possible title, then meet Jackson's eyes. "What do you think?"

Jackson puts down his phone, the video shoot over for now. "This is going to be sick—the song, the doc, all of it. I can't thank you enough, man. Letting me tag along to shoot videos? You are seriously a rock star. And that's no lie," he says with a wink.

I smile. "It's nothing."

He marches up to me and clasps a hand on my shoulder. "You've taught me a lot over the years, Miller. And one of those things is to be straightforward with your feelings. So, let me do the same—it's *not* nothing. It's everything."

I practically shuffle my feet. *Gee whiz.* This kid. Damn. He's one of the good ones. I knock his shoulder with my fist. "Anything for you, man. Anything for you."

When he takes off, I check my phone. Five. Ally is usually done working by now. I'm so jazzed to see her that I can't even waste time flirting. I need to know what she's doing and hope that list includes me.

Miller: Are you off work? What are you up to? I wrote a new song.

Ally: Just packing up for the day. I need to pick up Chloe from her friend's house in an hour and a half, then I'm taking her and Hailey out to dinner.

Miller: Full mom mode tonight, huh?

Ally: Seems that way. Did you want to talk later? About the song? Can't wait to hear it!

Miller: I don't want to talk about the song right now.

Ally: You don't?

Miller: I want to use my mouth for other things. Can you come over before you pick her up?

She doesn't answer right away. I pace, running my hand through my hair, muttering *c'mon*. A few minutes later, my phone buzzes. She's in the Lyft, and she'll be here in ten minutes.

I head straight for the shower.

Pretty sure I heard somewhere that women like it when a freshly showered man answers the door.

Or one woman does.

CHAPTER 22

Ally

The doorman knows me, and tells me Miller's expecting my arrival.

When I step into the elevator, I'm ready to bounce off the walls, to leap out of my skin. Everything in me is tight, coiled, ready to pounce.

All I can think about is sex.

And skin.

And lips.

As the elevator rises higher, I wonder if I've become a nympho in twenty-four hours. How have I spent my whole day trying to stop a reel of wildly erotic images of my best friend?

At the ninth floor, I ask myself if I felt this way from the night I met him.

At the tenth, I'm considering if this is the consequence of six years of longing bottled up and finally let loose.

At the eleventh, I nearly vault out of the lift, sprint down the hall, and rip his door off its hinges.

Calm down, girl.

I raise my fist to knock, and I hear the faint rumblings of his voice shouting, "Coming."

Make me come, I want to scream.

When he opens the door, I'm looking at the most delicious benefit of my whole life—Miller, dressed in nothing but a towel. It's white, slung low and tight on his hips, and reveals those abs and a hint of the V.

My throat goes dry. My eyes take a leisurely stroll along his carved body. A droplet of water slides down his chest, on a path between the grooves of his abs, stopping at the top of the towel. The wet ends of his hair curl. His face is scrubbed clean, but he hasn't shaved, and I could get down on my knees and thank him because I love his stubble.

Love the scratch of it.

And I love, too, that I've now experienced the absolute sensory delight of a man answering the door, freshly showered, sexily clean, wearing only a towel.

In fact, I like this sight so much that my brain shuts off every thought but one.

Touch him.

Stepping inside, I slam the door, drop my coat, hat, and bag to the floor, and push him against the wall. I crush my mouth to his. He groans instantly, and then louder still when I make my intentions clear. Grabbing the towel, I yank it off, then gasp. Half a dozen musical notes are inked on his hip. Small, pristine tattoos. Mesmerized, I run my finger over them, humming.

Humming "Love Me Like Crazy."

"You have your song on your body," I say, a little amazed.

His lips curve up. "I like that song. Right now, I'd like your hands on my body."

I wrap my hand around his hard-on. He growls.

I smile. "I believe it's my turn."

"Take it, baby. Take your turn."

I do, getting down on my knees as I stroke his steel shaft. I look up at him. His eyes are hooded, his lids falling closed, his Adam's apple bobbing.

"Fuck, baby. Let me feel that luscious mouth on me. Let me feel it now."

I squeeze his cock, and a drop of his arousal glistens on the tip like a pearl. A bolt of lust darts down my spine. I'm a woman with a one-track mind, and I flick my tongue across that bead, licking him up.

I moan.

He harmonizes with me, and do we ever make beautiful music as I dive right into the heart of the song, taking his gorgeous cock all the way into my mouth.

"Ally," he groans, threading his fingers through my hair. "This is what I pictured in the shower this morning."

A thrill zips through me. "You thought of me doing this?" I draw him back in, savoring the hitch in his breath as I suck.

"This. You. On your knees."

"What else?" I ask, eager for his dirty words.

"Licking you. Bending you over the bed. Fucking you on the pool table," he says, and a pulse beats between my legs as I picture all of the above.

His eyes start to close, and his jaw twitches. He lets out a feral moan as I work his cock with my mouth and hands, stroking the base and cupping his balls as I suck.

"I picture tying you up. Don't know why I want that. I just do."

I want *that*. To be tied up, pinned down, and fucked hard. Fucked raw. Fucked to the ends of my desire. I want to give in to everything I felt for him years ago.

Every single thing.

Including this. There's no weirdness, no

awkwardness. We're just two people burning with lust and giving in to it.

I drag my tongue along his shaft, taking him to the back of my throat. "Your lips, baby. Your lips are so fucking sexy. So fucking sexy I want to come all over them."

His words make me suck faster, tighter. I want him to come and come hard. I give the base of his cock a squeeze, and then one deep suck to the back of my throat, and he grits out an orgasm alert.

"Coming. Now." His body thrusts, then jerks to a stop.

Drinking him down, I let him flood my throat until he pulls me up, cups my cheeks, and stares at me with wild eyes. "How much time?"

He can barely talk, and I love it.

I glance at the nearby clock. "I need to leave in ten minutes."

He scoops me up and carries me to the piano bench. "This will help me finish the song."

My eyes widen in surprise, then I tremble when I see what awaits—a silver and red ribbon is draped over the piano bench.

"Early Christmas gift to me," he says wiggling his eyebrows as he tugs off my sweater, tank, and bra, then pulls down my jeans. I kick off my shoes.

I'm nearly naked in front of a man who's only ever been my friend, and a dash of nerves spreads over my skin. I want him to like what he sees. The way his breath hitches and his eyes blaze tells me all I need to know.

We both like the view of each other.

I hold up my hands in front of me, crossing them at the wrists. "Wrap me up, then."

He slides a hand between my legs, and I tremble into his touch. "That's what I wanted to know, baby. That's what I needed."

"To know I want you so much I can never wear these panties again?"

He smiles wickedly. When he cups me between my legs, the sound he makes is the sexiest thing I've ever heard. "This is my reward," he rasps out, stroking the obscenely wet panel of my panties.

My eyelids flutter. "For what?"

"For waiting six years to touch you."

I shake as he peels my panties off, leaving me naked before him. "Have you waited that long?"

He stares at me with a heat in his eyes. "The night I met you, I wanted to kiss you. I wanted to fuck you and make you come. And now I can."

My mind is nothing but a haze of lust as he guides me to the bench. I sit, and he raises my arms, ties my wrists above my head, and then lays my back against the keys. I'm not sure this is the most comfortable position, but I'm positive I've never looked sexier, since the floor-to-ceiling windows give me a view of myself—I'm spread out on his piano bench, my spine arched over the keys, a silver and red ribbon tied tightly around my wrists.

Miller kneels, places his hands on my knees, and spreads me open. I whisper his name in a desperate plea.

He breathes out roughly. "Look at you, baby."

He glides a finger through my wetness.

One touch.

And I'm hovering on the edge.

"You're so turned on for me, aren't you?"

"Yes."

Another finger joins, sliding through all that slickness, and stars flicker before my eyes. I think I could come in seconds.

He dips his face to my thigh and licks my skin. The sounds I make shock me. I've never whimpered like this in my life. I've never wanted anyone like this.

I never knew my Miller could do this to me—make me quiver. Make me practically sob with longing. Tightness threads through me, a pulsing need to be taken.

"Have you wanted me too?" His breath is hot on my skin, and already I'm in some other world, some world where truth and desire are unleashed like wild beasts running free. Have I wanted him? Hell, yes. But I've denied it. I've shoved it away. I've hidden it.

Now, as his lips skate so close to where I want him most, I don't deny.

I confess.

"I've wanted you so much." Words burst from my lips. "I want you to lick me and eat me and make me come on your mouth."

A groan seems to rip from his throat as he licks a line up my center like he's finishing the last taste of the most decadent dish he's ever had.

I'm wrecked. Completely wrecked.

He moans as he kisses me. He growls as he widens my legs farther. And his eyes fall shut in a look of the most intense pleasure I've ever imagined on a man. As he licks me, the pleasure electrifying, a truth hits me.

I've imagined him.

I pictured this that day back at the hobby shop, when he teased me about ribbons. I've flirted with it well before then too. But I always found a way to hide it.

There's no hiding anymore as Miller covers me with his mouth. I try to lift my hands, but I can't. "I want to wrap my hands in your hair and pull you close," I murmur.

He opens his eyes, winking as he flattens his tongue and licks, flicking the tip of it against my swollen center. I'm keenly aware of the ticking clock, racing perilously close to my exit hour. But I'm aware, too, of every exposed nerve ending, every inch of skin, every rippling wave of heat as Miller goes down on me.

I can't grab him like I want, can't yank him closer, but I can arch my back, lift my hips, and thrust against his face.

Oh God, I'm fucking Miller's face.

And it's filthy and divine.

I can't stop. Won't stop. I love the stubble scratching me, I love his lips on me, and I love everything about his wild abandon. As I rock up, he grips my thighs tight, devouring me like he promised. Pulses of pleasure ricochet through me until I'm there.

I chase down bliss, and then I find it. I come undone on his lips, so magnificently that my noises have to be audible across town.

And I don't care.

When I manage to open my eyes, Miller's standing, stroking his hard cock. It's like an iron spike.

"Look what you do to me, baby. When you leave I'm going to take care of this again."

"I wish I could stay for that," I say.

He bends to me, brushing his lips against my cheek. I murmur contentedly as endorphins wash over me, a beautiful wave cresting endlessly. He reaches my ear and kisses the earlobe. "I meant every word, Ally. I've wanted you for so long, and you taste better than cherries."

I shiver from the sheer sensuality of his words, but the stark truth scares me. I'm not sure what to do with all this want we've unleashed. What happens to it when our friends-with-benefits deal inevitably ends?

Because arrangements like this always end.

Maybe that's why I can speak the truth.

"I've wanted it too," I admit, since there's no point holding back. The cat's out of the bag when it comes to our lust—might as well embrace the truth while we reap the rewards.

There's no time to linger though, since I have to be downtown, so I rush to clean up and get dressed. Two minutes later, I'm standing by the door, grabbing my bag and coat. Miller's towel is back in position, and I want to rip it off again.

"We didn't work on the song," I say playfully.

"Such a shame."

"Send it to me tonight? We're booked for some time in the studio tomorrow afternoon."

"It's an easy arrangement. You'll have it down in no time," he says, punctuated by a rumble in his stomach that makes me laugh.

"Hungry much?"

He pats his flat abs. "That's what happens when you have dessert first."

I join in the ab-patting party. Because . . . why not? I slide my hand over his belly. "You better eat, hot stuff."

He shrugs happily. "Want company picking up Chloe? I can get ready quickly."

His request throws me, and I don't answer right away.

He furrows his brow.

"Well, it's just that I'm taking Chloe and a friend out," I say.

"I don't mind."

But the funny thing is . . . I do. And I'm not sure why, but maybe because tonight feels different than last night. Yesterday was an unexpected and fantastic exploration. Today was deliberate. I need to wrap my head around how to balance bandmates, friends with benefits, and the unusual role Miller plays in Chloe's life.

I need to do that before the lines blur any more.

I wince, wringing my hands. "I feel like she'll know we were doing something."

"She's eleven."

"That means she knows basic stuff."

He holds up his hands in surrender and fixes on his toothpaste smile. "No worries. I have tons of stuff to do here, actually," he says, gesturing grandly to his living room.

"I'm sorry," I say softly, then raise my chin. "I just need to figure out all this . . . *stuff*."

Yes. *Stuff.* That's a euphemism if I've ever used one.

"Go," Miller says, flashing me his winning grin.

"Bye," I whisper, then rise up on tiptoe to cup his cheeks and kiss his lips. He's tense for a sliver of a second, then I feel him melt against me, sighing into my mouth.

I want to hold on to this feeling, but more than that, I want to know what the hell to do with it.

CHAPTER 23

Ally

Hailey swishes her chicken satay into the peanut sauce, then takes a bite. "And did you see when Maddie tried to switch things up with her sister?"

Chloe's eyes twinkle as they dissect the latest episode of their favorite show. "And it worked. Until the disco ball fell down. Oops!"

The girls laugh in tandem, then Chloe scoops up some pad thai noodles with her chopsticks, smiling the whole time.

Hailey's eyes pop out, cartoon-style, and she points as if she's spotted a unicorn trotting down Broadway. "Oh my God, you can use chopsticks! I want to learn."

Chloe tips her head to me. "Ally taught me. They're so easy once you know how to do it."

Hailey grabs her chopsticks and thrusts them in my direction, batting her eyes. "Teach me, please."

"Of course. It's easy-peasy." I can see why Chloe likes Hailey. The pixie blonde is animated and full of positive energy.

I teach her the basics, and a few minutes later, she's clumsily twirling noodles into her mouth.

"You're amazing," she says to me. "You're like the mom on *Girls Rule*. She's super cool too."

That's high praise, so I smile and say thank you. As they return to the issue of whether Maddie should let a new drummer into their all-girls band, my mind wanders to my own bandmate. To how Miller looked so hurt, then tried to cover it up so valiantly.

Was I cold for putting my foot down about dinner?

Or was I wise?

I sigh as I take a sip of my tea, wishing for answers, wishing I knew where to even look for them.

But I don't, because I don't have a knitting pattern to follow with him. We're not dating, but we are screwing around, and it's only temporary, and yet we're still friends. I wish I'd been able to give him a yes to something as simple as joining us for dinner.

The last few times I tried to integrate men I dated with my family, it didn't pan out. Miller's different, of course. But what does it mean that this man who's played a key role in Chloe's life for several years is now also the man I'm enjoying benefits with?

Temporary benefits.

"Would that even work?" Hailey's question interrupts my reverie. "Would it be possible for somebody who sings soprano to hit those low notes?"

We're back to the topic of *Girls Rule*, as Hailey lays out the scenario the lead singer faced in a recent episode. I weigh in with my musical opinion, then the girls ask if they can order mango sticky rice for dessert.

"Since the first semester is almost over and I've done well in school," Chloe says, making her case.

"Me too. It can be like a reward," Hailey adds, and they're like two puppies, vying for an extra scoop of kibble.

"Let's do it."

After we finish the sweet rice and I pay, Hailey grabs her phone to text her mom, while Chloe rests her head on my shoulder. "Thanks so much for doing this, Ally. I had a really fun time."

A neon light flashes brightly in my brain. *Ally.* She called me Ally for the first time. I blink, my mind tripping back to earlier at dinner. She called me Ally then too, didn't she?

I sit straighter, a question poised on the tip of my tongue.

But Hailey looks up from her phone. "Can you sleep over tomorrow? I just asked my mom, and she said it's fine with her."

Chloe's eyes plead with me from behind her glasses. "We have a half day, and then winter break starts. Can I, Ally?"

Third time. I beam. I don't know why it feels like I've graduated to the next level, but it does, and I'll take it. I'll happily take it. "Absolutely."

While we walk Hailey back to her apartment, I'm on cloud nine, and I want to share the news with Miller.

Later that night when Chloe's asleep, I text him, but there's something else I need to say first.

Ally: I missed you at dinner, but I'm not sure how to balance everything now.

Miller: *gif of juggler with ten pins in the air*

Ally: Seriously though . . . I should have invited you, but I'm trying to figure out how to make everything fit.

Miller: *gif of cat sliding under a bureau*

Miller: It's all good. I NEVER want to pressure you when it comes to Chloe. I was just starving. You know me and my appetite.

Ally: Yes, I do.

Miller: But I do understand that the juggling is real for you. And that you have to do what makes sense.

A familiar feeling rushes over me. It's how I felt the other night when I saw Miller carrying Chloe. It's the feeling of falling. He understands, and he's so good to both of us.

Ally: So I'm forgiven?

Miller: That would imply you did something bad. Were you a bad girl, Ally? Oh wait, you were naughty. Please do more naughty things.

And we're good, so good, so I move on.

Ally: Want to send me the words and music for your new song?

Miller: Check your email. ☺

Ally: I see it! Also, I'm no longer Aunt Ally.

Miller: WHAT???? Are you OK?

Ally: Gah! Didn't mean to freak you out! It's all good. She doesn't call me Aunt Ally anymore. It started tonight. Apparently, I'm just Ally now!

Miller: That is completely awesome!

I sink back onto my couch, open the email from him, and dive into the song, singing softly to get the feel for his new tune. Once I have the basics down, I grab my knitting bag and work on Sam's hat, still humming. As I work the row, I decide that I'm doing okay with Chloe, despite having to figure things out on the fly.

Maybe I deserve a reward too.

Even if I don't know right now how to knit Miller, Chloe, and me into any sort of pattern that makes sense, I know one thing: I want to see him again, and I've been given a golden chance.

Ally: Chloe is sleeping at a friend's house tomorrow night. Would you like to spend the night with me?

His response arrives faster than any message I've received in my life.

Miller: *gif of nerdy dude in glasses pumping his fist and shouting YES*

As I finish the hat, I decide maybe we can manage it all—Hot Stuff, and friendship, and benefits.

After all, what could possibly go wrong?

CHAPTER 24

Ally

I suck.

I flub so many lines I'm ready to send myself back to high school. I have factions of robots waiting to take over a zombie-infested school in the not-so-distant future, but the last few chapters of the sports-radio teen star story are killing me.

"Can't win 'em all," Kristy says with a shrug when I mispronounce *horrors* as *whores*.

I bang my forehead on the desk. "That word is a horror," I mumble into the mic.

"Could be worse." Kristy's voice booms in my headset. "The author could have used *peculiarly*."

Raising my face, I clutch my cheeks and gasp, like

I'm screaming in a slasher flick. "Never *peculiarly*," I say, since that's cruel and unusual punishment to a hard-working voice artist.

I take a deep breath, count to three, clear my mind, and then return to the final chapter, giving my all to the character as she comes to terms with being a girl who loves sports radio in love with a boy who wants nothing to do with a ball, a field, or a racket.

With laser focus, I nail the ending.

It's two hours later than I expected though, which knocks me off schedule for starting the undead tale. Plus, Miller's going to be here any minute, and we're supposed to rehearse.

I check my phone for any change in plans, and an email message blinks at me.

Extra pickups needed for the Casey Stern book. Sorry! But we want to wrap it up before the holiday break.

It's Angie at Butler Press, and I call her back. "Hey, I'm at my regular studio. Can I do them here?"

She pauses before answering, and that's a clear no. "Well, if there's any chance you can just scoot up here, we'd prefer it. We really want the same sound environment."

What the client wants, the client gets. "I'm on my way. See you in thirty."

I wave goodbye to Kristy, call a Lyft, and ring Miller on my way down the stairs.

"What's a five-letter word for where I plan to spend the rest of the night?" he says as he answers.

A laugh bursts from my chest. "I have no idea. *Couch*?"

"Nope. *Inside you.*"

I count off. "Miller," I say, deadpan. "That's nine letters plus a space."

"Oh, excuse me. I meant p-u-s-s-y."

My jaw drops. "You're filthy."

In an ever-so-innocent voice, he says, "I spelled it out."

"Oh, well, then you're a cupcake."

"I'd like to eat you like a cupcake."

I laugh, since I don't think I'm going to be able to call up the serious side of my friend right now. "I have to head to Butler Press for an hour. I'm going to be late for rehearsal."

"Then I'll hang out longer with Campbell. We're having lunch."

A kernel of worry digs into me. "Are you talking this way in front of him?"

"He's in the little boys' room. Don't worry. I'd never say words like *I want to fuck you till you come hard, scream my name, and beg me for another* in front of him." Miller pauses. "Oh, hey, Cam."

I blush at his antics. "Miller," I chide. "Does he know you're talking to me?"

"Hi, Ally," I hear Campbell say.

I sigh, then whisper, "Does he know?"

"That I always talk to you like this? Yes."

Since I'm not going to get a straight answer out of a most-festive Miller, I switch gears. "I won't be back at the studio to rehearse for another hour, hour and a half. Can we push our rehearsal back? I checked, and the studio is open." But before he can answer, an idea hits me. "Unless you want to go start with Campbell? Rehearse it with him till I get there, and do any final fine-tuning?"

"Brains, beauty, and a plan. If I'm ever trapped on a desert island, I want it to be with you."

"Let's hope we're only trapped for a day or two, because I'm terrible at fishing."

"Me too. I'm excellent, however, at using UberEats."

As the car slogs uptown, something occurs to me. Tonight's a desert-island kind of night, and I want Miller to know how much I want to be stuck with him on that island.

Since I'm quite skilled at using UberEats too, I order him a surprise at the studio.

CHAPTER 25

Miller

When I hang up with Ally, Campbell shoots me a look across the table at Willy G's, his favorite diner. "So you need me to save the day?"

"Yes. Can you ride in on your white horse, please?"

"But of course. I save my loyal steed for occasions like this."

"Seriously though. You want to help me for an hour or so? Unless you have a lesson."

He shakes his head. "My schedule is your schedule." He glances around to make sure no one is listening. "Don't repeat what I'm about to say."

I press a finger to my lips. "Your secret will be safe

with me."

He whispers conspiratorially, "I don't hate playing with you."

I toss a french fry at him. "Thank you. Thank you very much for the not-hate."

"You're welcome. And the truth is, it's the opposite of *not-hate*."

"Thanks. I *not-hate* playing with you too."

He grabs his Diet Coke and downs some, then clears his throat. "Also, what's the deal with you and Ally?"

I do my best confused look. "What do you mean?"

"Gee, I wonder?"

"Spit it out, bro."

He scratches his jaw. "Call me crazy, but I picked up on this vibe from the two of you at my house, and from the way you were just talking to her. Is there anything more?"

I take a breath and debate whether to tell him, but in my hesitation, he finds the answer.

He smacks a palm on the Formica. "I always knew the two of you could be something. Glad to see it took me for it to happen."

"First off, nothing is *really* happening. We don't want to mess with our friendship. Second, you're taking credit?"

"Hell, yeah. I love credit. Also, how exactly is the

not-really-happening part working out for you?"

"It's going . . ." My voice trails off as I debate how much to say, then I decide to err on the side of he's-already-figured-it-out. "It's going as well as a friendship can go with a woman you've wanted for six years."

"Ouch."

"Yeah, exactly."

"That sounds like I need to pay." He plunks down some cash for the bill, and I can't argue with that.

We skedaddle from the diner, heading for the studio.

When we arrive, the receptionist smiles at me with her wide eyes. "Mr. Hart, there's a delivery for you."

She hands me two cups from Dr. Insomnia's. One is marked *C* and one is marked *M*. I lift the plastic top on *M* and my mouth waters when I see hot chocolate, topped with extra whipped cream. There's a note on the cup too.

From A . . . No dongles were harmed in the making of these titular beverages.

I laugh, my heart flipping around in my chest as I take a drink, then once more as I hand the coffee to my brother, loving that she sent a drink for him.

He takes a sip then lets out a low whistle as we walk down the hall. "You have it bad, Miller."

I consider denying it, but what's the point? I kind

of do, and that's both awesome and awful at the same time. I shrug, take another hearty gulp, and say hi to Jackson, who's waiting in the studio.

Then we get to work on making music.

Music is where I don't have to think, don't have to figure out too-complicated-even-for-the-SAT problems. Music comes naturally to me, and it fulfills me in a way nothing else can or will.

I show my brother the music and the lyrics for "Coming Together," and it takes him all of a minute to get a feel for the song. Campbell grabs a guitar that's resting against the wall, slings it on, and strums the first few notes.

I sing, and something is just easy about playing with him. Even though I wrote the song to sing with Ally, even though it doesn't suit two male voices, I still feel the rush I experienced when I was ten and we formed our first band in the treehouse in our backyard.

Campbell smiles too, nodding his head as we make melodies, and it's better than instinct. It's a beautiful summer breeze.

It's only when I look up later in the session that I see we have an audience. Ally, Kristy, Jackson, and the receptionist are watching us from the other side of the glass, clapping and cheering.

"Oh, stop," Campbell says into the mic, but his smile says *keep it up*.

"It's not often we get to see the Heartbreakers jamming," Ally says from the other side.

"It's not often it happens." I used to try valiantly to get him to start up again with me, but he's always said no. I've accepted that Campbell doesn't want to play again in the band. But a song or two now and then seems to suit him.

"Want to play it again?" he asks.

"Hell, yeah."

When we jam through it one more time, Jackson's camera on us, Ally's eyes watching thoughtfully, I savor every second, content to enjoy each moment and make the most of it.

After Campbell says goodbye, Ally joins me in the studio. "You know it'll never sound the same with me as it does with him," she warns me.

"It's not supposed to sound the same. It's supposed to have our mark on it," I whisper in her ear.

She trembles, and I take that as my cue to tell her something else. "This is going to be the hardest rehearsal of my life, because I can't wait to get out of here."

When she smiles at me, I know.

I fucking know.

I've fallen for my best friend.

Too bad I have no clue how to get off the desert island with our friendship intact.

CHAPTER 26

Miller

It's not just the hot chocolate. Or the fact that she leaves Bananagrams out on the coffee table and gives me a cute, flirty look, like we're really going to play it tonight.

It's not even the new bottle of wine she left on the kitchen counter.

It's the menu she made.

Once we step inside her home that evening, she hands it to me—a sheet of white paper, folded over. The front of the menu reads: *Tonight's specials.*

I arch a brow as I open it then peruse the offerings.

Ally with ribbon
Ally undressed
Ally bent over the couch
Ally naked and under you in bed
Also, wine, Bananagrams, hot chocolate, Skittles, and
more treats are available à la mode, as are crazy conver-
sations; ab explorations; long, lingering kisses along your
jawline; nibbles on your earlobe because that drives you
crazy; and any combination of blow job, hand job, 69, or
anything else upon request.
By the way, I recommend starting with an appetizer of
hot, wet kisses.

I close the menu. "Get over here."

She comes up to me, and I cup her cheeks, stare into her sapphire-blue eyes, and brush my thumb along her jawline.

"I'll start with one order of hot, wet kisses."

"Coming right up."

I twist my fingers in her hair as our mouths collide, and she gives me the most delicious serving of my life. Our tongues skate together, and our lips seem to know precisely what the other wants. It's a dizzying kiss, filling my brain with a static haze.

With my hands still in her hair, I walk backward

with her to the bedroom. That's where I want her, her breath coming fast, her skin flushed.

I disengage from her mouth when we reach the pristinely made bed. The red polka-dot ribbon I gave her snakes its way down the white comforter like an invitation. I grin wickedly as I flop down on the mattress, pulling her on top of me. Cupping her ass, I grind her against my hard-on. "Did you like being tied up yesterday?"

She nods, her eyes shining with desire. "So much."

"Why?"

She wriggles against me as I kiss the curve of her neck. "I like the way you make me feel when you tie me up. I like giving you control."

I groan and yank her closer, curling a hand around the back of her head because I can't stop kissing her. First, the corner of her mouth, then her jaw, and at last I travel to her ear, nibbling on her earlobe.

She murmurs as I go, her voice as soft as a feather. "But why are you so intent on tying me up?"

That's a damn good question. I lick the shell of her ear as I contemplate the answer. Why do I want that so badly?

Because I want her . . . I want her all to myself, and probably some caveman part of me wants to make her mine. Because I feel so fucking much for her that sometimes tying her up is the only way to contain those feelings.

I flip her over and proceed to strip her, unzipping her jeans. "Because you're so fucking beautiful when you let me do what I want to you," I say, telling her a half-truth.

"Do what you want to me," she whispers, and I nearly die of lust. Combust from it.

Tension rattles through me, hot and urgent. I want Ally to know when I touch her, when I kiss her, that I'm not like anyone else who's come before.

I'm the kind of guy who'll stay.

For her.

For her kid.

Only she's not ready to hear that, so I'll let my hands and mouth and desire do the talking.

We undress in a flurry, sweaters, shirts, jeans flying off. But when she's down to her bra and panties, I slow my pace, stopping to admire her. I drag the tips of my fingers from her breasts down her soft belly, savoring the sight of her pink panties and matching pink bra.

"My Honey Lavender likes pink." I nip her hipbone.

"I do, but I also like wearing nothing with you."

I groan as a bolt of lust slams into me. She sits up, reaches for my hips, and slides down my briefs.

Another carnal moan escapes my throat as she

wraps a fist around my length. This woman. Her hand. Her eager touch. I could have her every day and be happy.

I close my eyes and rock into her hand as she strokes my cock. She has a firm, tight grip as she moves her palm from tip to base. Yes, I could definitely be happy for all my life. I let my imagination wander—nights like this, days with her.

When she whispers my name, my eyes float open slowly. "Yeah?"

"I'm clean and on the pill. Can we go without a condom?"

My dick twitches, throbbing impossibly harder in her hands. "Same. I'm clean."

She loops her hands around my shoulders and falls back on the bed, bringing me with her. I roam my gaze along her lovely frame, then my hands catalog her beauty. Rose-tipped nipples, a freckle on her belly, a scar from her appendectomy when she was ten, and the softest skin I've ever felt. When I spread her thighs open, lust charges through me as I see how wet she is.

How ready for me.

She lifts her fingers, running them over the musical notes on my hipbone.

I settle between her legs, rubbing the head of my cock against her heat. Arching her back, she whimpers, murmuring my name in a half-begging voice.

She's a live wire, and touching her is the best thing I've ever done.

I shudder at the thought of *not* doing this again.

But thought is drained from me when I push inside, sinking into her welcoming paradise. I still myself when I'm all the way in, my breath stuttering, my pulse skyrocketing.

Pleasure sparks along my skin, and my dick hums the happiest tune in the world. This is where we both want to be. Bracing myself on my elbows, I lock eyes with the woman who's been by my side for the last several years.

My best friend.

My new lover.

It's all too much, and not enough at the same time. She's gazing right back at me, vulnerability etched in her blue eyes. And something new too.

I want that something new.

Surrendering to the feel of this kind of bliss, I move inside her, trying to say with my body what she means to me. That I love fucking her because I'm fucking the woman I've fallen in love with.

Some good it did trying to stay just friends. Maybe I was never just friends with her. Maybe I've always been racing to *this*. Toward flushed skin and urgent kisses. Toward arched backs and needy whimpers of *yes* and *more* and *so good*.

She laces her hands tighter around my neck, tugs me closer, and brings her lips to mine.

"Miller," she whispers before she kisses me hungrily.

I've been racing toward her.

Toward my name on her lips as she chases the edge of desire. I want to take her there. I want to be the only one who ever does.

Swiveling my hips, I rock into her, every nerve ending in me crackling. She matches each stroke, and we move together. We kiss together. We say nothing together, and our silence speaks volumes.

We're always talking. Joking. Laughing. Saying dirty things.

But if I open my mouth now, I'll tell her how I feel.

I swallow the words, keeping them to myself till I know she can handle them. Till *we* can handle *us*.

I kiss her neck, then go deeper, so deep she's writhing and begging, her breath speeding up, her eyes squeezing shut. She moans my name, and it's never sounded as good as it does when Ally's coming apart beneath me.

Relentless pleasure blares through me, a euphoria that signals my orgasm isn't far enough away.

But I want more for her.

I want her too far gone. I grit my teeth and

somehow stave off my own climax so I can flip her over to her hands and knees. She's still trembling, still moaning softly as I push her palms toward the pillows. I grab the ribbon, wrap it around her wrists, and tie the ends to her headboard.

She looks at me, biting her lip. "Take me."

If she only knew why I need her like this. Because I've wanted her for years, and when I sink back into her, it occurs to me that maybe I've been falling in love with her for six years too.

Six years.

And now I'm here, and all this touching has unlocked all these feelings.

Feelings I don't know what to do with.

So I do as asked.

I take her.

I want to take her and keep her, and I know that as I fuck her, I'm making love to her.

It can never be anything else with my Ally, my Honey, my woman.

Soon, she's nearing the cliff again, then she's soaring off, crying out, and I give in too, as pleasure barrels down my spine, curling tight in me till I come hard inside her.

The ecstasy blots out the complete and absolute mess in my head.

CHAPTER 27

Ally

I order Vietnamese like a champion, and then we play Bananagrams as we wait for the delivery, making it through four words before we kiss again. The kiss lasts a few minutes, then I sink to the floor, bring him into my mouth once more, and treat him to another blow job as he sits back on the couch, moving my head up and down between his legs.

When he comes, my cell rings, and it has to be the food delivery. Flailing my arm, I grab for the phone, checking the number, then hand it to Miller.

"Yessssss," he says on a final moan as I suck him dry. "Come on up."

Perfect timing.

We eat, then we drink wine, then we return to my bed, and he kisses me everywhere. I'm pretty sure I'll be sore tomorrow, and I'm pretty sure I don't care about anything but the way he treasures my body.

I run my fingers over the inked notes on his hip, humming a few words from one of the Heartbreakers' most popular songs. "*All I want is to find you again . . .*"

A slow and peaceful grin spreads on his face, and he answers me, crooning softly, "*Even if that's crazy.*"

My thumb slides higher over the artwork on his body. "*Tell me, tell me . . . I haven't lost you.*"

He beats out a gentle rhythm on my belly. "*Tell me I'm not crazy.*"

I cease the singing. Maybe because it's not our song. Or maybe because it's skating perilously close to words that might overwhelm this fragile thread between us.

* * *

As the night crawls past midnight, we slide under the covers, and we don't stop.

We are wild, hungry creatures, needing more. More contact. More touch. More of each other.

I pull him on top of me. "I like every position so far, but I really like looking at you, Miller."

"Baby," he groans, and closes his eyes as he enters me.

I wrap my legs around his hips, bringing him as close as I can. Our slick, sweaty bodies slide against each other. In the dark, in the absolute bliss detached from all reason and responsibility, the hope inside me dares to swell again. The way he touches me makes me feel so rich with love that I want to blurt out everything. To tell him I want him in my life every night.

When I'm scarily close to breathing the most dangerous words, he goes so deep in me that I see heaven.

My brain turns into a delicious haze of lust and love as I surrender once more, and he joins me. When he tugs me against him, and I curl into his arms, all I want is to let this perfect night stay absolutely perfect.

Once the sun rises, I'll find a way to make sense of the emotions occupying all the space in my heart.

For now, I have Miller's arms around me.

My refrigerator is a desolate wasteland. My belly is the maw of a shark, growling and chomping.

"How is this possible?" Miller scratches his head as he considers the empty shelves that mock our rumbling morning tummies. His rumpled hair after a night in my bed is adorably sexy, and I riffle my hand through the strands. He harrumphs as he paws at a loaf of bread nearing the end of its life. "Why do you hate food so much?"

Laughing, I park my hands on my hips. "I'm a New Yorker. I've found all the cheap takeout and delivery in the city. It's an art form that makes the fridge irrelevant."

He squeezes my ass. "But don't you know you have to have eggs and coffee for your man after you fuck him senseless?"

I imitate a ruler, standing straight and tall.

My man?

He means *my friend*, right?

He rubs the pad of his thumb across my cheek, taking my focus away from dissecting the finer meanings of his words. "How about we take a quick shower and grab a bagel? You can feed me that way."

I nod quickly. That, I understand. Bagels are what we've always done. That's the breakfast of friends.

I glance at the time on the stove. "Let's be speedy. Chloe should be back in an hour, then I'm taking her to Brooklyn to spend the day with Kirby and Macy while I finish some work."

He points to the bathroom. "Get your cute little ass in the shower."

* * *

As he washes my hair with strong but tender hands, the questions return.

Are these the hands of *my man*?

Or *my friend*?

Or *my temporary man*?

My head says "friends with benefits," but my heart screams something else entirely. Something I can't quite make out over the rushing of the hot water.

When he rinses my hair, I decide to broach the subject in a roundabout way. "I like the hair washing. Is this another benefit?"

I turn my head, meeting his gaze briefly. He blinks, furrowing his brow, then he flashes a smile. "Of course."

And that's no help.

In the back of my mind, I hear the clock ticking. We haven't discussed an end date to this arrangement. But there has to be one. "Friends with benefits" comes with an expiration.

Just like our band does.

My heart sinks as I put two and two together. I've known this all along. But I never let myself truly consider when this newfangled deal would end.

Miller is a short-term kind of guy. He didn't even want to commit to singing with me for longer than a month, so it's no surprise that this deal will be incredibly short too.

He clearly didn't mean anything more when he said he was my man. Just like when he turns me against the wall, pushes my palms to the tiles, and slides his fingers between my legs—that doesn't mean anything more than a fast track to temporary bliss.

Even as he whispers sweet nothings in my ear.

You feel so good.

I could do this over and over.

This is the best way to wake up.

They are merely weightless words. They have no anchor to tie them to the future. They're part of our deal, and deals always end.

Even so, his words try to trick me, so I do my best to quell the riot in my heart when he whispers, *Love the way you feel in my arms.* Fortunately, forgetfulness is easier when an orgasm overwhelms me, pulling me into its euphoric haze.

After we get dressed, we head down the stairs. Wrapping my scarf tightly around my neck to brace against the chill, I let the door to the building fall shut behind me and walk straight into Chloe.

And Hailey.

And Hailey's mother.

"Hi, Ally." Hailey speaks first.

I freeze on the sidewalk, my eyes widening like

saucers as I regard the three of them. Am I wearing a sign that says "I got laid last night when my kid slept at your kid's house"?

Not that there's anything wrong with that.

But still. It's kind of . . . tacky.

Shucking off the invisible slut-shaming sign, I call on my best rogue princess warrior, raise my chin, and say good morning to Hailey's mom, who I met the other night. "Good to see you again, Jesse."

"Good to see you too."

"Mom, Ally taught me how to use chopsticks the other night," Hailey says.

"That's great," the equally blonde and just as waif-life Jesse says with a smile.

"And Hailey, this is Miller. He taught me how to make a castle." That's Chloe's contribution. She squeezes Miller's arm, and he drapes it around her shoulders, squeezing back.

"Good to see you, Monkey."

Jesse's eyes stray to the man by my side. He's wearing jeans, boots, a sweater, and a telltale sign that he's not *just a friend*.

The ends of his hair are wet.

I pat his shoulder, drawing on my best cool confidence. "Miller's a good friend."

It feels like the truth, so help me God.

But it's also a two-faced lie.

"Nice to meet you, Miller," Jesse says, extending a

hand, and the two shake and exchange brief pleas-
antries.

Jesse turns to me. "I'm sorry to bring her back so
early, but I forgot I have to take Hailey to the dentist.
You know how it is with winter break. You try to jam
everything in. I tried to text you to let you know we'd
be coming early." She smiles sweetly. "The message
must not have gone through."

She's the most darling woman, covering for my
fuck-up. She has to know I missed the message
because I was getting busy with the man I introduced
as a friend.

"I must've missed the text," I say with a gulp.

"No worries. I'm glad we caught you. We'll see
you again soon." Jesse turns to Miller, then me, and
lowers her voice. "Are they, or aren't they?" she whispers, wiggling her eyebrows, and I wait for the sidewalk to open up and suck me into an underground
pit of embarrassment. She returns to a normal
volume. "I saw your videos. They're so good. Like
those ice dancers." She blows out a stream of air and
fans her face, as if she's burning up.

She gives Miller one last glance. "Also, I loved
you as a Heartbreaker."

When she leaves, I'm officially a beet.

* * *

Chloe doesn't seem to notice or care that Miller spent the night. Probably because she believes me when I lie to her, saying that he came over this morning to meet me for bagels.

The lie tastes bitter.

It's the opposite of all the ways I've tried to raise this beautiful girl. When we finish our food, I gesture to the nearest subway stop. "It's off to Brooklyn we go."

"I'll tag along," Miller says. "I told Miles I'd stop by to see him and Ben before they left for London, but he's not expecting me till the afternoon. That cool?"

"Of course." I don't hesitate this time—it's a chance for me to redo the dinner invite snafu.

But I don't know if this means anything special, or if this is just us back to the way we were, shuttling Chloe around town, having breakfast, being part of each other's lives.

My head is a muddle. We could be one thing, we could be another. We might be friends, or maybe he's my man. We're this or we're that.

I want to shut down the noise, turn off the dial on the radio. But my brain is loud and persistent, stuck between two stations, and it can't tune in clearly to either one.

On the train, Chloe tells us about her sleepover

and the fun they had. "Dr. Jane would be happy for me."

I smile. "Of course she would."

Chloe pumps a fist. "But I don't have to see her again. Because I'm not a broken plate anymore."

"You never were, Monkey."

When we're off the train, she practically skips to Kirby's building. "I can't wait to see Aunt Macy and Uncle Kirby."

Those two titles for them make my heart bounce with delight, like a child frolicking through a field of flowers. But before she goes inside, she stops and hugs Miller. "I'm glad you're not leaving."

"Leaving? Where would I go?"

She shrugs. "I don't know. London, Boston. Somewhere."

He tucks a finger under her chin. "Don't worry. I'm not going anywhere."

"Good. You're always around, and I like it."

A warning bell rings. I recall what she said a few nights ago, her sadness over Kirby moving to Boston. I'm glad she's expressing her feelings. I'm thrilled she's sharing her heart with people she cares about. That's one of the reasons she went to see Dr. Jane in the first place. To find her voice.

But part of her expressing them means I need to hear them.

You're always around and I like it.

That means something.

That means everything.

The chill in the air intensifies. But there's a biting chill inside me too. I shiver painfully, my teeth chattering, as I say hello and goodbye to Macy and Kirby, telling them I'll be back at the end of the day.

Miller and I return to the station. The grime from the platform wafts up, a nose-crinkling stew of pee and rats and garbage. The train arrives, and we step inside. As it rumbles out of the station, I heave a sigh. "That was awkward."

"What part?"

"All of it," I say heavily. "Jesse. Hailey. The whole thing. Could we have been any more obvious?"

"But Hailey's mom was cool about it."

"She was, but I was at a loss for words. I mean, what was I supposed to say? This is my friend who I screwed last night?"

He winces. "Ally."

I drop my head into my hands and sigh. My stomach churns. My gut twists. My collar grows too tight, and everything in me squeezes, like I'm being wrung out by two hard fists.

Chloe's words echo in my mind.

You're always around and I like it.

But other words resonate too.

Expiration date. Friends with benefits. Make a deal.

And still more, the voice of Dr. Jane, urging Chloe to speak her mind.

I raise my face. I look at Miller, take out my sword, and prepare to do battle with reality. "When do we end?"

He flinches. "What do you mean?"

Like my heroines, I charge forward into the fray. "When do you want this to end?"

Say never. Please say never.

He swallows and nods a few times, as if he's processing what I just asked him. When he answers, the words come out flat. "When do *you* want this to end?"

That's my answer.

His isn't a never.

His is whatever works for me.

I want so much more, and he wants only a moment.

Someone has to put her foot down. "We wanted to get this out of our system, right?"

"Right," he says, his voice sounding emptier than I've ever heard it.

I swallow roughly, soldiering on. "Maybe we should go back to how we were, before it gets too hard."

That's what a strong girl would say. That's what a fighter would do.

Give up what she wants for the greater good.

He scrubs a hand over his jaw, stares out the scratched window, and parts his lips to speak.

But he says nothing.

One minute passes. Then another. Finally, he nods. "Yeah, totally. That makes perfect sense. Let's go back before it gets too hard."

When we reach my destination, my heart is a bruised peach at the market, and everything is already too hard.

CHAPTER 28

Miller

I've got this. I've handled moments like this before.

Well, not exactly like this. I've never had my heart smashed by a wrecking ball.

Also, thanks a lot, Miley Cyrus, for stealing that idea for a song.

But since I can't write "Wrecking Ball," I'll do what I've always done when things don't go my way: dive into a new activity.

What would that be? I drum my fingers on my thighs, hunting for inspiration on the goddamn subway train.

That's it.

I smile faintly, because the answer was so easy. I

turn to my phone, calling up Google. Twenty minutes later, I'm walking along a quiet block of New York City in the East Eighties to a model train shop.

When the Heartbreakers split, I took up, well, everything. Soccer. Kickball. Lacrosse. Jigsaw puzzles. Monopoly. Yes, there are Monopoly leagues.

I also worked on mastering fantasy basketball, baseball, football, and many other sports. I don't need to work. I have enough money for a few lifetimes, thanks to our royalties. But I like to have fun, and that's how I've kept busy.

That's what I've done when the other bands I've played with broke up too. I've found the next thing to do.

Today, I'm confident it's going to be trains.

Everyone loves to play with trains.

The bell rings above the door to the shop as I stroll inside.

"Happy holidays." A man sporting a thick gray beard and a conductor hat looks up at me from his perch at the desk, where he's attaching wheels to a caboose. "What can I do for you?"

I clasp my hands together like I'm embracing the sheer genius of my plan. "It's time for me to invest in a train set."

"Join our club." He rubs his hands together, wanders around the counter, and gestures to the small, cramped shop. "Let me show you some options."

He regales me with details of model trains, how to take care of them, how to assemble them. When he's done, my head hurts. Too many details. Too much work.

I don't have any interest in building a train set.

But this guy has made a helluva effort. He deserves more than, "Thanks, but no thanks."

Spinning around, I point to a starter set for a five-year-old. "That one, please."

It'll be Ben's Christmas present. With the model train set tucked under my arm, I head over a few blocks to a sporting goods store. I buy a foosball table I'd checked out a month ago. I ask for express delivery in an hour. After it arrives at my pad, I take a deep breath, square my shoulders, and dive into the solution to the Ally heartache.

This table will cure me.

It'll numb the pain.

Hell, it'll do more than that—it'll make me happy again. I don't like being unhappy. Not one bit.

I play, beating myself several times. I start another round, turning up the volume on my speaker system, blasting Muse's "Madness."

When the song ends, I don't feel any better.

My chest is hollow, like someone has tunneled through it with a shovel and scooped out my insides.

"Fuck," I say, as I spin one foosball rod aimlessly. Dragging a hand through my hair, I stalk around the table, wishing I could invite Ally to join me.

I want her here.

I want her back where she's been.

But I've no clue how to return to Friendship Land.

I fiddle with my phone, flicking through my contacts. Campbell probably has a lesson, Miles has a meeting with his financial manager before he takes off tonight, and Jackson is helping his mom today.

It's just me and my shadow.

I sink down onto the piano bench. The piano is always good company. The piano has always been a friend. I tap out a few notes, and soon I'm playing "Piano Man," and hell, if there's a number that's better designed to amp up sadness, I don't know what it is.

When I play the final note, I drop my head on the keys.

I might as well work through all of Depeche Mode and The Smiths.

I want Ally, and I can't have her.

After all these years, I understand what it means to be a heartbreaker. Or, really, I understand what it is to be heartbroken.

CHAPTER 29

Ally

Robots keep me company. Zombies fill my hours.

And so does a plucky, determined girl named Stella who must navigate her way through a dystopian future populated by those warring factions.

I do my best to put myself in Stella's shoes, and at the end of the day, I pat myself on the back. That was one of my best acting jobs ever. I acted as if I wasn't completely shredded inside.

I never realized how far the arrow of Miller had bored into my heart. Once you let someone in like that, let them touch you, let them kiss you, let them see inside your soul, they have the power to hurt you.

My muscles hurt. My cells ache. I don't get headaches, but I have one today since I've been caging in tears for eight hours straight.

But the pain is my fault. Miller didn't hurt me. I hurt myself by messing with one of the best things I've ever had. I messed with our friendship simply to scratch an itch.

Maybe I should be a robot. Then I wouldn't have to deal with stupid things like lust, and what it can sometimes lead to.

Love.

A love that I don't know what to do with.

As I head to the elevator, I say hi to Meg at the reception desk as she packs up for the break.

"Happy holidays, Meg."

"And to you too, Ally." She wraps a scarf around her neck. "By the way, who sent you that gift the other day?"

"Just a friend."

Who I love madly.

Meg arches a brow from behind her big glasses. "The guy you've been singing with?"

"Yep."

She laughs to herself. "Girl, he doesn't look at you like a friend."

I try to laugh it off, like this is a performance and I must be convincing. "Oh, the videos are just us performing. We're really *only* friends."

My stomach twists saying that out loud because I wish I were lying. I wish we were so much more than friends.

She shakes her head. "I'm not talking about the videos. I'm talking about the way he looks at you when he's here."

I step closer to her, intrigued. "How does he look at me?"

"Like he wants to find you under his Christmas tree."

That image tugs at my heart and, inconveniently, at my loins too.

"And like he wants to keep you," she adds.

My heart crawls up my throat. That's such a crazy thought that I have to dismiss it.

I give a small shake of my head. "See you in the New Year, Meg." As I press the button for the elevator, I check my email to distract myself.

A new message from Angie at Butler Press sits at the top of my inbox.

Thank you so much for coming in yesterday. The file sounds fantastic, and it's a wrap! Keep your fingers crossed, but I think we might have something new and exciting for you in the New Year.

I tuck my phone into my purse and cross my fingers for a moment.

This email is the reminder that I needed to keep my focus on work, on shoring up my business and planning for the future.

That's how I'll get through my gig with Miller this week, and that's how I'll get through . . . everything.

Even though Miller is how I've gotten through everything else that's come before.

* * *

When I arrive in Brooklyn, I haven't done anything but think about how it felt to be in Miller's arms last night, the way he kissed me, and all his sweet and tender words and gestures.

Foolish heart.

It's a heavy heart too, an anchor in my chest weighing me down.

Must focus on something else.

As I walk to Kirby's home, I catalog his neighborhood—the pickle shops, the organic dry cleaner, the parents carrying babies on their chests.

The trick works momentarily.

When I reach his house, Kirby tells me Macy and Chloe are on their way back from the park, and the baby's sleeping.

"Tell me stuff. Are you excited for the move?" I ask in the most chipper tone I can muster as I flop onto his couch amid the packed boxes.

"Definitely. It's going to be a great opportunity." He tilts his head, studying me. "Um, you don't look so hot today."

I slump against the cushions. Leave it to a brother to see through your armor. I could tap-dance around his observation, but I've sung and danced all day, and it's exhausting. "I don't feel so hot."

"What's wrong?" He sits next to me, a worried crease on his forehead.

A sob—the one I've been holding in since the morning— works its way up my throat. I choke out the truth. "I'm an idiot. I went and fell in love with my best friend." The tears escape, and Kirby wraps an arm around me and shushes me.

"It's okay. It's going to be okay."

"It's not going to be okay. We're not you and Macy."

He shoots me a quizzical stare. "Why can't you be Macy and me?"

"Because you guys are the exception. Falling for your friend doesn't usually work out this well," I say, gesturing to the house, to the life he shares with Macy. "Miller's the best friend I've ever had, but he's not the type of guy who wants to get serious."

Kirby clears his throat, scoffing at me. "He's not?"

"He's not," I insist, hiccupping.

He scratches his jaw. "Didn't he come with you this morning to bring Chloe here?"

"Yes."

"Doesn't he help you with Chloe's school projects?"

"Yes," I answer, wondering where he's going with his questions.

"Don't you go to his house, and have dinner with his family, and hang out with his brothers and their friends?"

"But that's because we're best friends. Of course we do that stuff."

He shoots me a look. "Seriously, Ally?"

I toss my hands up. "Yes, seriously. That's normal friends stuff. That's what I don't want to lose."

Doesn't he get it? I want to keep Miller in my life, and friend Miller is better than no Miller.

Kirby arches a brow. "I think it's something more. Something deeper. Honestly, I've always thought there was a spark between you two."

"You have?" My heart beats a little faster. I can't let myself believe that, but oh, how I want to.

"You guys have always seemed like you like each other."

I can't hold it all in. "Yes, fine. Okay. You got it out of me. Something happened. Something happened a few times," I say, spilling out all the messy thoughts in my head.

He laughs lightly. "I didn't even ask, but good to know I was right that you'd leveled up."

"But it can't work."

"Because you think Miller can't be serious. But my point is he *can*."

I let out a moan, like air seeping out of me. "But . . ."

"But I'm right. You've been friends for six years. That sounds like he knows a lot about commitment. It sounds like he's been there for you for a lot of things. And it sounds like maybe he has some of the same feelings you do. I don't think he'd mess around if it was just physical."

I take a beat, trying to insert this new puzzle piece into the jigsaw of today.

The problem is I can't slide the piece in around this little girl who's mine to take care of, to raise, and to love. I don't want to disappoint her. More than that, I don't want to hurt her. "But what about Chloe? I don't want to set her up to have another person leave her life." Then I whisper quietly, my voice shaky, "And I miss Lindsay."

"I miss her too," Kirby says softly, reaching for my hand and squeezing it. "We'll always miss her. Chloe probably will too. But you can't protect Chloe from everything, and you definitely can't shield her from ever getting hurt again. She'll get hurt. She'll cry. She might like some guy you date, and she might dislike some other guy you date. That doesn't mean you shouldn't try."

But what would trying with Miller even mean? Asking him to date? To be my boyfriend? Does anyone even use that term anymore?

Hey, Miller, wanna be my boyfriend?

I'm so rusty I haven't a clue.

I don't feel like I know anything anymore.

Usually, I am strong, determined, and fierce, like I've skimmed a little off the top from the badass heroines I narrate.

Today, I'm just a girl who's crying in her brother's arms.

* * *

"Does that sound like a good idea for tomorrow?"

I force myself to focus on Chloe over dinner at home. She's detailed what she wants to do tomorrow, her next day off.

Smiling broadly, and ever so falsely, I tell her that her idea sounds great.

With her fork poised in midair, she stares at my face, studying me. "Why are you in such a funk?"

Ouch. Called on my mood by my girl. "Robots and zombies took a lot out of me."

She spears a piece of pasta. "Maybe you should talk to Miller. He always cheers you up."

She's right. I should talk to him. After all, how else are we going to return to the way we were?

CHAPTER 30

Miller

As the sun dips low in the sky, I swing by Miles's hotel room at the Luxe, doing my best to shove my loneliness out of my head.

For the record, loneliness sucks.

I like people. I like companionship. And I like these two knuckleheads.

"I guess you two cats didn't exactly trash your room like rock stars," I tease, surveying the suite. It's immaculate. "Wait." I wag my finger. "What's that?" I ask, pointing to an empty package of Goldfish crackers and a carton of milk on an end table.

I spin around and wiggle my eyebrows at Ben.

His eyes widen, and he purses his lips like he's sealing in a secret.

Oh, hell. The kid is guilty of something. "Looks like someone did party like a rock star," I tease.

Miles strides across the plush carpet, picks up the empty packages, and tilts his head. "Ben, what did I tell you?"

Ben's expression drops like he's been busted. Only I can't imagine what for.

"Is he not allowed to have Goldfish and milk?" I ask, scratching my jaw. "That's kind of harsh."

"It's so harsh," Ben says, stomping his foot.

Miles huffs and answers both of us. "He's *allowed* to have milk and Goldfish. He's *not allowed* to order them from room service without my permission."

My hand flies to my belly, and I crack up. "You called room service to order milk and Goldfish crackers?"

"Daddy was in the shower. I was super hungry. Haven't you ever been super hungry before?"

"Little dude, I'm super hungry all the time." I bend to one knee and ruffle his hair, then turn to my brother. "If you have a five-year-old who already knows how to call room service, your life is a good life."

Miles relents somewhat. "I know. It's not a big deal. But I have to have some rules. Some expectations, you know?"

I nod. "Sure. I hear you."

Miles sets a big hand on Ben's small shoulder. "Of course you're going to be super hungry at times, and I don't even mind if you call room service. But you know the rules. You just have to ask me first."

Ben's bottom lip quivers. "I'm sorry, Daddy. I'll ask you next time."

Miles beams. "I love you, little man, and that's why I have rules for you."

"I'll do a better job following them. I promise."

"I know you will."

Ben offers his hand to shake. "It's a deal."

"I accept your deal." Miles takes Ben's hand and yanks him in for a hug. Seeing my little brother so affectionate with his son, as he's always been, makes my heart kick. He's done everything for his boy, all with no mom on the scene.

"I love you to Pluto and back," Miles says.

"I love you to infinity and beyond."

"I love you to the depths of the oceans and all the way to the sky."

It's too sweet, and I need some of that loving. I need a contact high. "What am I? Chopped liver? Give me some of that sugar."

Ben rushes over and hugs my waist. "I love you, Uncle Miller. I'm going to miss you when we're in London, but I know I'll see you again soon. The tour is only a few weeks."

"You'll see me soon. That's a promise, and I love you too. I love you like crazy."

Miles chuckles.

I meet his gaze. "And I love you too, Dodgeball. Don't let anyone ever tell you otherwise."

As his suite at the Luxe becomes a gigantic love-fest, an idea knocks on my skull. A little tap at first, then louder, more insistent. It's fueled by these two knuckleheads and the way they love.

All I need now is a plan.

Fortunately, there's a date on my calendar that feels perfect for a target.

CHAPTER 31

Miller

Part of the plan is making sure Ally knows I'll always be her friend, first and foremost. Even if we never become anything more, I want her to feel the same certainty with me that Ben feels with his dad.

I want her to feel safe and confident.

I text her that night.

Miller: At the end of time, is it best to be aligned with robots or zombies?

Ally: Talk about a hard question . . . Battling both

was exhausting. Ultimately, zombies are the worst. (PS: I was just about to text you.)

Miller: PS: Mind meld. Also, zombies are absolutely the worst.

Ally: But robots are quite totalitarian. So pick your poison.

Miller: I'll take door number three, please.

Ally: Good choice. Also, it's really nice to hear from you.

Miller: Did you think I would disappear?

Ally: Honestly?

Miller: Why would I want you to be anything but honest?

Inside, though, I'm a coiled ball of tension. I hope to God she knew I'd text—just because our benefits arrangement ended, it wouldn't change my role in her life. I need her to know I'm not simply fun-and-games Miller. That I'm the guy she can depend on.

Ally: Honestly, I never doubted it. Or you. But I also still LOVE it.

She didn't say she loves *me*. But loving it—hearing from me—is a good start.

Miller: I'm glad you know you can depend on me. Also, I have big news here at Casa Hart!

Ally: Tell me, tell me!

Miller: I scored a foosball table.

Ally: Finally! Can't wait to play it.

Miller: You have an open invite.

Ally: And did you say goodbye to Miles and Ben?

Miller: Yeah, and I miss them already.

Ally: Aww. Hopefully, they can visit again soon. Also, I want to tell you something.

Miller: Speak now, please. :)

Ally: I like being friends with you. I was sad today, missing what we'd had. But I'm glad to know we can still talk like this.

Miller: You can count on me, Ally.

Ally: Same here. You can count on me, Miller.

I slump into my couch pillows, a little pang in my chest over the prospect of being just friends with her. But I sit up again, because I need to be happy with just friends. We might only ever be friends. And I'm going to be fine with that, even though I want more. For now, I start to tap out *goodnight*, but another message from her pops up.

Ally: OMG, did you see this?

Miller: See what?

Ally: Gah! This is the cutest thing ever!

I wait for her reply, willing it to come faster. What is she talking about? Otters holding paws? A cat playing the piano? Come to think of it, that would be impressive.

I swipe my thumb over the dial pad to call her when a video appears in my text.

The thumbnail looks like it's from a coffee shop. I hit play, and I'm transported back to the day Campbell and I listened to auditions at Dr. Insomnia's before playing an impromptu number that the woman who wore the maroon hat caught on camera. She'd said she wouldn't post it, but I guess she caved.

As I watch, I smile, because Ally and I are going to sing that song in two nights at our gig. I let my mind replay all the times we've sung it before. All the times we've sung other songs, both covers and originals. There's something there. Something more than chemistry. More than an itch that needed to be scratched.

I go to YouTube, and I look up one of Ally's most famous videos—when she and Kirby sang "Can't Help Falling in Love," mashed up with "Somewhere Over the Rainbow."

What if we could be a mash-up—friends and lovers?

There's only one way to find out.

CHAPTER 32

Ally

I reread the texts the next morning.

They're just texts, but they're also so much more.

They're Miller and me being, well, Miller and me.

They tell me we *can* go back to the way we were.

But when I shower, I remember Miller's hands in my hair, and when Chloe and I board the subway, I recall every time I've taken the train with him. When we walk toward Bryant Park, and I think of all the times Miller has met me here, there, and everywhere in this city, I know my brother was right.

Miller's committed, and so am I. Sure, our

singing agreement might have a deadline, but our friendship never has. *We* never have. And if I don't let him know I want this new us, we'll never get the chance to work out if Miller and Ally could be a couple with no deadline.

But how the heck do I tell him?

Do I send him a letter? Knock on his door? Do a tap dance?

I push the thoughts aside to zero in on Chloe's project.

"I think the lion is going to be perfect," Chloe says, as she angles closer to the statues guarding the building entrance and snaps a photo. She shows it to me on the screen on the back of her camera.

I give her a thumbs-up. "I heartily approve."

We're at the New York Public Library because she wanted to take pictures of it for her photography class, and because she wants to check out a book.

She grabs my hand as we head up the steps. "Can you recommend a good young adult story? You might know one or two."

"Just a few." I chuckle. "What are you in the mood for? Dystopian tales? Space battles? Epic sagas of magic and vengeance? Contemporary teens dealing with everyday loss and love?"

Her green eyes twinkle. "The last one. Ideally with a heroine cool like you."

"Ooh, cool like me."

"I speak the truth."

"Keep speaking it," I say, and as we head inside, Chloe takes more photos.

Once we check out several books, we wander down Fifth Avenue, passing a Christmas display at a boutique.

"Do you know what you're getting Miller for Christmas?" she asks.

"Nope. Any ideas?"

"You could always get him Skittles. You could get him a lifetime supply of hot chocolate. Or you could get him a new version of Bananagrams, since he likes all those things."

"Santa could hire you as an elf."

"Or you could get him something else. What's the thing he wants most in the world?" she asks as we stop at a light.

Instantly, I know the answer.

I do some research to confirm my theory. I want to be certain. I also want to be armed. Like a lawyer, I prep to make a case before the jury of one. I gather my evidence. I call upon my best witnesses.

The first order of business is to visit Mackenzie.

She's not even surprised when I tell her my idea. "It's brilliant," she declares.

But she's not the only one I need on board.

Fortunately, if there's one thing I've learned from all the books I've narrated, it's that a heroine must line up her troops. We head across town to Murray Hill—Chloe, Mackenzie, and me. Campbell is teaching a violin lesson, but Samantha is home. She's making cherry jam cookies for her Instagram show, and they smell mouthwateringly good.

I tell her my idea.

She claps and practically bounces to the ceiling, like a spring-loaded Tigger.

Then we execute the plan, and if this works, there's a certain person who's going to be out of his mind with happiness tomorrow night.

* * *

When I kiss Chloe goodnight, she's still a little giddy from our secret plans. "I love your idea, Ally. Will you text me as soon as it happens? Unless you've changed your mind and I can come to the show?"

"Sorry, Monkey. You'll have fun at Hailey's. I'll text you, though, as soon as it happens."

She hugs me, and I feel a sense of peace. I can't save her from the world, but I can make sure her world with me is safe.

I've decided to stop worrying about my ability to take care of her. I'm doing a fierce and fabulous job as her parent.

And nothing and no one will ever change that.

CHAPTER 33

Miller

At the club the next night, I smooth a hand over my T-shirt in front of the mirror in the men's room.

"Shoulda worn a sweet suit, man," Jackson says, sweeping his eyes over me.

"I'm a T-shirt kind of guy."

"I know, but sometimes you need to break out the swank. A silver blazer and sleek black pants."

"I would think that'd make it obvious. I want some subtlety."

"Fair enough. You are one subtle rocker, then, and you rock a T-shirt."

He's seventeen so he shouldn't be here, but the

owner made an exception for his documentary, and has required Jackson to wear a plastic bracelet so no one serves him as he shoots videos.

I looked down at my outfit. Jeans, motorcycle boots, and a T-shirt. It's how I dress. I want to be myself. I want to be the guy that I hope Ally wants.

When she arrives, she's Honey Lavender. Blonde glam wig. Luscious top. Pouty lips and dark eyes.

But it didn't take her dressing as Honey for me to fall in love with her. It took her convincing me to sing with her. It took getting close to her like that to make me realize she's the one I've wanted all along.

I feel like I've drunk ten cups of coffee, and I don't like the stuff. But I'm amped up and jittery, hoping she wants all the same things I do. Hoping I'm not wrong in thinking she might.

As we head to the stage, I whisper, "We have a crowd."

She nods nervously, wringing her hands.

"Hey," I say softly, reaching for her arm. "It's going to be great."

"It is," she says, as if she's reassuring herself.

We head onstage, and I introduce us quickly. "I'm Miller Hart and this is Ally Zimmerman, and together we're Hot Stuff. And this is our first number."

We slide into our original tune, "Maybe." We sing

it like we did at the studio, like it's only us. We sing like Virtue and Moir skate, like we want each other. Based on the cheers and hollers, the audience likes us as much here as they do online, and I'm stoked.

My eyes take a most enjoyable stroll up and down Ally's body, savoring the chance to drink her in. I stop at her waist, and blink—she wasn't wearing *that* before. The red polka-dot ribbon I tied her up with the other night is playing the role of a belt.

Kill me now.

I move closer and wrap a hand around her hip, fingering the silky fabric of the ribbon. Tugging her near to me, I brush my lips along her neck, and the audience goes crazy. They love how we are together.

I love how we are together.

And I hope to heaven and back that she feels all the same things. I pray that the way she trembles in my arms isn't simply because the song is sexy, but because we are sexy together.

And because we should be together.

As soon as the song nears the end, I'm ready to lay out my heart. To tell her before the whole crowd that I want to go all in. I want her and Chloe, a package deal. All strings attached. I want rules and expectations. She doesn't think friends with benefits is a good idea, and neither do I. I want more, and by showing her this way, by declaring it in front of the world, I hope she sees that I'm a risk worth taking. That we're more than benefits.

We're a sure thing.

But when the music ends, she walks offstage.

CHAPTER 34

Ally

My heart pounds in my throat. Nerves speed through the freeways of my body as I dart from the stage like a runaway singer. Mackenzie waits for me in the wings and takes my hand. Her smile is radiant.

"Did Miller look shocked?" I ask.

"Completely."

"And what about . . .?"

"He feels great. I think seeing Miller sing with you has dredged up memories of how good it can be when you find your perfect singing partner. He was missing this kind of chance. You've given it to him."

My heart beats a million miles an hour, and I

want so badly for Miller to understand that I'm not walking away from the band.

Even though I am.

What I'm really doing is giving him his heart's true desire.

When I watched the video from the coffee shop, and the one from the recording studio earlier in the week, and then my mental replay of how the brothers sang together at Campbell's apartment, I knew that this is what Miller truly wants.

Mackenzie and I reach the dance floor in seconds, as Campbell strides onto the stage. Taking my place, he strums the most familiar opening chords in the history of the Heartbreakers.

Miller's smile isn't the toothpaste variety now, and it's not the naughty one I've seen after-hours. It's the blue sky on a crystal-clear afternoon. His face is a thousand sunny days.

I practically jump for joy, loving that the happiest guy I've ever known is now even happier.

My own smile spreads to the moon and back as I cheer so loud my voice will be hoarse tomorrow. I'm not alone. Everyone is shouting and screaming. This is what it means when a crowd goes wild.

They might have liked Miller and me. But this is true love. This is when music is magic and a love that lasts through all the years.

CHAPTER 35

Miller

It's happened. Science fiction has warped with reality, and I've entered an alternate universe.

One where my brother Campbell is jamming onstage with me.

Not in front of the kids at Christmas, but before a motherfucking audience. What the hell is happening?

He flashes me a grin. I have no clue what's going on. But I go with it, because that's what you do when you perform. We do it in style, belting out "Love Me Like Crazy."

The audience hollers, and their energy is bigger and brighter than it was when I was here with Ally minutes ago. This is an epic cry of excitement. Of pure glee.

I have no idea why Campbell's here, but I'm having a blast singing the tune we wrote when we were sixteen and seventeen, jamming in our garage at our home in Jersey after convincing our parents they should let us be a band.

We don't sing it to each other, all sexy and hot like Ally and I do. *Please.*

We sing it to the crowd, like we've always done. That's what they want. That's what I want too. There's something special in the air. When I play with Campbell, the magic isn't in how we look at each other. It's in the music, and how we make the music together. It's coming home.

This is what I've longed for, and even if this is all I get—one song with Campbell—I'm going to savor every single second of it.

Because of how I feel. *Overjoyed.*

I pour all that joy into the song, and the crowd can feel it. I can feel their joy, like we're trading off, sharing the most epic emotion.

I'm pretty sure Ally can feel it, because she's right there at the edge of the stage, singing along. Singing all the words we sang to each other in bed.

But this time, we finish the lines.

"*Don't you love me like crazy?*"

This wasn't how I planned it. I was going to tell

her onstage how I felt. I wasn't going to do it through this song. But plans change, and I can't wait.

I switch it up. I change a word as I gaze into her eyes. "*I love you like crazy.*"

"*I love you like crazy,*" she mouths to me, a wild grin stretching across her face. That grin makes my heart jet to the stratosphere.

When we finish, I'm made of nothing but adrenaline and the wish to have this woman for the rest of my days. I grab her hand and pull her up. The crowd is chanting and cheering, but I have blinders on, and eyes only for her. "Ally Zimmerman, I love you like crazy."

CHAPTER 36

Ally

"I love you too. So much," I say as tears streak down my face. A dam bursts. I've been holding so much in, and I can finally say it all.

He cups my cheeks. "I love you, and I love Chloe, and I love the package deal, and I want it all. I want all in with you. Will you have me?"

I gasp, and I try to speak, but my throat is clogged with emotions. They're overflowing in me. I didn't expect he'd tell me he loved me tonight. I wasn't sure he felt the same at all.

"Say yes!" someone from the audience shouts.

"What do you say?" he asks again, a smile on his

face, his hands on my cheeks, his forehead touching mine.

I'd say I'm floating. I'd say I'm falling. I'd say this feels so unreal.

"I want to be your man. Do you want me?" he asks.

"I do," I blurt out through tears of joy. "I want that so much."

My skin is buzzing, my heart is galloping, and the entire world is singing love songs tonight. "I love you, and that's why I wanted to give you this gift for Christmas."

"What gift?"

Campbell plays another note, the start of another song. "Coming Together." It's the one Miller wrote for us, but it sounds so much better when he sings it with his brother.

I grab his mic and turn to the audience, collecting myself. "Ladies and gentlemen, what would you think of the Heartbreakers getting back together?"

A momentary hush falls over the crowd, and seconds later, the silence spins into a roar.

Jackson captures every second on video, and I couldn't be happier that he's nabbed an even better story than before.

As Campbell plucks out the chords, I whisper to

Miller, "I knew this was what you wanted more than anything. I want you to be happy. I want you to play with your brother. So I asked him, and he said yes."

He stares at me with mad love in his eyes. "I love you so fucking much."

CHAPTER 37

Campbell

For the record, I've been thinking about getting the band back together for a while.

How could I not? Miller's been asking me for a long time. He's been wanting to reunite since we broke up. I didn't want to then. I didn't even want to a few months ago.

But it took a certain woman. Or really, two women. Wait, make that three women.

Mackenzie, my daughter, and Ally.

They didn't convince me, per se. Instead, they showed me the way. Yesterday, when Ally, Mackenzie, and Sam sat me down, they played me the video from the coffee shop, and Ally asked, "How did you feel then?"

As I watched, I remembered having an absolute blast with our impromptu song. It felt right and good to sing with Miller. I couldn't contain my smile when I answered her question. "Happy. I felt happy."

Mackenzie squeezed my hand. "And how about when you sang with your brothers in front of the Christmas tree?"

I'd pictured the three of us around the tree, rocking out to holiday tunes, and my heart somersaulted. "I loved it."

"And you guys both have notes from the same song tattooed on your body," Ally added. "From your first hit song."

"Are you saying that's a sign?"

Mackenzie laughed as she shrugged. "You told me you had the tattoo done ten years ago. That was *after* the band broke up. Miller had his done *afterward* too. Maybe you've both been missing it. Maybe it was meant to happen again."

The more she'd shared, the more spot-on her observations felt. They'd resonated inside me.

Then my daughter had played the clip of us singing "Coming Together" in the studio.

That was the final lightbulb moment. In that clip, I looked like I was having the time of my life. Fact is,

I've always loved playing with Miller, and with Miles too.

Even years after we'd split, I'd savored the little moments when we had a chance to sing together again.

But it wasn't till I saw those moments reflected back that I realized there was an ache inside me too. A longing to have that once more, but to have it be different this time around.

"What if you could have that again?" Mackenzie suggested.

I looked to Sam, swallowing hard. "I don't want that crazy life."

"Dad," she said. "It doesn't have to be crazy. You guys can do it on your terms, like Ally and Miller were doing it on their terms. Be local and do online videos. The internet is where the action is, anyway."

I keyed in on one word. "*Were?* You and Miller *were* doing it on your terms? Does that mean you're done, Ally?"

She shrugged, but it was a mostly happy one, with only a hint of sadness. A lone tear rolled down her cheek. "You guys were meant to play together."

I scrubbed my jaw, considering her suggestion. Could I still play with the guys in the Righteous Surfboards? Sure. Why not do both? Could I still teach? Of course. It's my life, and my schedule. And could I play with my brother again, making videos for the Web and playing shows in New York City?

"Can I do this?" I asked Mackenzie.

A huge smile spread across her gorgeous face. "Campbell, it makes you happy. And Sam is fourteen. You don't have to worry about her. Plus, you have me to help. We're a family."

My heart soared like a hot-air balloon. Could there be a more awesome woman by my side? I curled a hand around her head and kissed her.

"Dad!" Samantha squealed.

I moved away from her and shrugged. "What can I say? I love her, and she's right."

As I've been learning, the women in my life are usually right.

Then I gave them my answer.

Hell to the yes.

Now, I turn to my brother. "Want to get back together?"

He laughs. He smiles. He can barely speak. All he manages is a raspy, "Yes," followed by, "Am I dreaming?"

"It's real," someone shouts from the audience. "Play 'Hit the Road.'"

My brother and I finish out the set to thunderous applause.

* * *

Miller

I didn't see this coming. I had no idea she'd do something like this. When the show ends, I find her in the wings, back her against the wall, and kiss her senseless.

"This is the coolest thing anyone has ever done for me," I say once we come up for air.

She beams, her fingers playing with the hem of my T-shirt. "I wanted you to have what you wanted most."

"I do want this." I reach for the belt loops on her jeans, then her ribbon, bringing her close again. "But you're wrong, baby. You're what I want most."

She wriggles against me. "Then have both. You can have me, and you can have this. Package deal."

"Like you and Chloe?"

She nods and smiles, the kind that can't be contained.

I press another kiss to her lips, then another, and one more. "You're my best friend, my lover, and my girlfriend, and I will look out for you and for Chloe because I'm going to be there for both of you. You know that, right?"

"I do," she whispers.

I arch a brow, wondering what this means for Hot

Stuff. "What about you? You don't want to perform with me still?"

She shakes her head. "Why don't you and I focus on being together and being in love?"

I can't argue with that, so I don't even try.

* * *

Later that night, I show Ally all the ways I love her. I tell her all the things I didn't say the other evening. I slide inside her, whispering words of love.

If I thought the first time with her was out of this world, I was wrong. This is galaxies better, because when you can both say *I love you*, it's simply the best.

Afterward, I run my hand through her hair. "So, we'll pick up Chloe tomorrow morning. Together?"

She laughs. "We will."

"Can we tell her we're a thing?"

Smiling, she answers, "I think she's going to be quite happy."

"I think so too."

The next morning we take Chloe out for breakfast. Over pancakes, Ally clears her throat. "There's something we need to tell you. Miller and I are involved now. We're a couple."

Chloe snort-laughs. "It took you long enough."

EPILOGUE

Ally

I wrap my hands around a mug of tea and take a drink as Chloe searches under our little Christmas tree for a gift.

"Hmm. What should we open next?" she asks.

With my slippered feet tucked under me, I peer at the Christmas loot, hunting for a pretty green box containing a silver necklace I bought for her. It has a camera charm on it, and I hope she likes it.

"Miller, can you grab the green box with the silver bow?" I ask.

"Ho ho ho," he says in a deep voice, and Chloe laughs. Then he whispers something to her. She nods excitedly.

"Don't tell her what's in it!" I chide.

A chuckle comes from Chloe, who covers her mouth, saying nothing.

"Found it," Miller declares.

"Wait," Chloe cuts in, grabbing another gift I can't quite see. "You forgot this one from Santa, Ally."

I set down my mug on the coffee table and wait to see what Chloe wants to give me from the jolly man in red. It's a small white box with a red bow.

"Santa is so smart," Chloe says.

"He really is. I wonder what he brought me," I say, but really, I wonder what Miller bought me since he must be pretending to be Santa for her sake.

I unknot the bow, rip open the paper, and freeze.

My lips part, and wild hope rises in me. It's a blue velvet box.

This can't be . . .

I blink as I click it open, gasping when I'm blinded by a stunning diamond.

In a split second, Miller's down on one knee, taking my hands in his. "Ally, you're my best friend and the woman I adore. I've been falling in love with you for six years, and I don't want to wait any longer for us to have this beautiful life together that I know we can have. Will you marry me?"

"Oh, my God. Oh, my God. Oh, my God." My soprano voice hits a new high, and tears rain down.

Chloe claps and squeals. "Is that a yes?"

I laugh and cry, throwing my arms around Miller. "Yes. I want that more than anything."

"Good." His eyes find Chloe's. "I want us all to be a family."

"We already are," I say.

"Then this makes it official." He slides the ring on my finger, and it's stunningly beautiful.

I hug him and kiss him chastely. Chloe jumps on the couch, sliding in next to me and staring at my ring. "I helped him pick it out."

I laugh. "You're an amazing ring elf. And you two worked fast."

She leans her head against my shoulder. "Can I give you a gift now?"

"Of course."

Chloe hands me a package, and when I open it, I find her smiling selfie inside. Only it's not alone. She framed a picture of all of us in the coffee shop, with whipped cream on our faces.

"I love it. It's perfect." I give her a kiss on the forehead, then rub my hands together. "Okay, let's see what else Santa brought."

Chloe drops a hand on my knee. "Ally, I need to tell you something."

"What is it?"

She takes a deep breath and fixes me with a serious stare. "I know Santa is really my mom."

She thinks Santa is Lindsay? Oh God. I'm going

to need to call Dr. Jane again. "Chloe," I say quietly, but Chloe continues.

"Everyone knows that Santa is your parents." She points at me. "So you're Santa."

My hand flies to my mouth. My eyes widen to moons. I can barely speak. As she roots around under the tree for another gift, I turn to Miller, mouthing, "*She called me Mom?*"

He nods. "Merry Christmas, Ally."

I have more gifts than I ever expected, since I have everything I've ever wanted right here.

ANOTHER EPILOGUE

Ally

I scurry around my room, hunting for my favorite red sweater.

"Chloe, have you seen my red sweater? The one with the little pearl buttons?"

"No, but your phone is ringing," she shouts from the living room.

"Crud. Can you answer it?" It's probably Miller, but I'm going to be late to the New Year's Eve party if I can't find my sweater.

Seconds later, Chloe appears in my doorway. "Sure, Angie. She's right here." Chloe covers the phone to whisper, "Angie from Butler Press."

I startle. She's calling me on a holiday? I grab the

phone as I fling open my bureau drawers. "Hey, Angie. Happy New Year."

"It will be if you can say yes to a huge new opportunity."

"Tell me what it is."

As I hunt through my closet, I nearly drop my phone when she makes me an offer—an offer that's going to do more for my future than a band would ever have done.

Just so I'm clear, I ask her, "You want me to be the voice for the lead singer in *Girls Rule*?"

Chloe shrieks, and I can barely hear Angie, but I make out enough. "Butler Press is owned by the same media conglomerate. The lead actress on the show has some vocal problems, and while she can still act on camera and do the speaking bits, she can't handle the singing. So when they were looking for a voice actress to record the songs, I thought of you immediately. We need someone who sounds like a teenager and has a gorgeous singing voice. That's you."

And as Chloe bounces on her toes, I say yes to being the voice of the lead singer in an all-girls band on TV.

I don't regret that I'm not being hired to be sexy, or to read a romance novel. They don't need my vocal gymnastics.

I've won a job by being who I am.

* * *

A little later, we're at Campbell's toasting the New Year with the whole crew. Jackson is here with a Diet Coke, and I congratulate him on winning the scholarship.

"It's a dream come true," he says.

Sam passes out cinnamon eggnog, and Roxy chats with Mackenzie over cookies. Chloe plays Bananagrams with Kyle, and this is officially the best life ever. Miller slides up next to me, wraps an arm around me, and kisses my cheek. "Nice ring, future Mrs. Hart."

I laugh. "Am I taking your stage name rather than your real name?"

"Ally Zimmerman, Ally Hart. All I care is that you're mine."

"I'm yours," I whisper. "In fact, maybe we can convince Chloe to stay the night here, and you can take me to your place and use that ribbon you like so much."

He growls in my ear. "Happy New Year to me."

We kiss again, and I'm so glad we sang together once upon a time, and I'm so glad it didn't work out. It's better this way.

As the clock ticks closer to midnight, there's a knock on the door.

"Who's that?" Campbell asks as he strides to the door. "Everyone's here."

"Everyone's not here," a familiar voice shouts from the other side, "until you open the door."

When Campbell unlocks the door, Miles strides in, a grin on his face, his son's hand in his.

Campbell brings in Miles for a bro hug. "Good to see you, Dodgeball. What are you doing here?" When he lets go, he scoops up Ben and ruffles his hair.

Roxy gives a little wave, smiling. "Yeah, I thought you were in London?"

"I was, but I have a reason to be back." Miles parks his hands on his hips and pins his gaze to Campbell's. "You didn't invite me to the party."

"You were across an ocean," Campbell says, as if he's trying to sort out what his little brother is talking about.

Miles laughs. "I didn't mean *this* party."

Miller strides over to his brother, saying hi and clapping him on the back. "What party, then?"

Miles points to his brothers. "I hear you're getting the band back together. Did you forget someone?"

My jaw drops.

Every jaw drops.

"Are you serious?" Miller asks, wonder in his voice.

Miles grins. "I want in."

The guys tumble together for a brotherly hug, and when they let go, Miller strides up to me. "And I have you to thank."

Seems like all the Heartbreakers are getting back together, and I can't wait to see their first show.

As I glance around at my family, I catch a look between Roxy and the youngest Heartbreaker, one where she smiles at him and he can't seem to take his eyes off of her. I wonder if this next phase of Miles's life is about to get a lot more interesting and complicated.

Something complicated doesn't have to be bad though—like how friends can be lovers, no matter what anyone says.

I turn my gaze back to Miller, and he drops a kiss to my lips.

Technically, nothing in life is a guarantee, but the way I feel when my fiancé kisses me once more tells me otherwise.

We feel like the surest of sure things.

THE END

Ready for more rock stars? Dying to know what's up

with Miles and Roxy and their stolen glances? Read all about it in the falling-for-my-brother's-friend romance **Once Upon A Wild Fling**! It releases on Oct 8 and if you liked Miller and Ally I think you'll fall in love with Miles and Roxy! You can order ONCE UPON A WILD FLING everywhere! I'd love to hear what you think of these books! Feel free to drop me an email at laurenblakelybooks@gmail.com and be sure to sign up for my newsletter to receive an alert when my next **books are available!**

There are a million reasons why Miles Hart isn't the man I should date but allow me to enumerate the top three.

He's friends with my brother, he's a single dad,

and he's a sexy, in-demand rock star. He might as well wear an off-limits, totally unavailable, and don't-even-attempt-to-ride-this-ride sign.

And there's one more, little itty-bitty thing -- he's never asked me on a date.

That is, until he asks me to be his plus-one when his band plays at his high school reunion. It shouldn't be a big deal. After all, we're just friends, and no one is giving us our own hashtag. Except me . . .

***

I have three good reasons to keep my hands off Roxy Sterling—her brother's my business manager, my kid is the center of my world, and the last time I fell hard for a woman I was burned so badly that my interest in relationships has gone up in flames. But once I bring Roxy's body next to mine on the dance floor, I want all the not-safe-for-work things I can't have with her.

My brain knows there's no way for us to work, but tell that to my big mouth. Because the second she plants a hot, sexy kiss on me, I have the bright idea to ask her to keep being my plus one—turning one night into a few.

What's the harm in spending a little more time with her and having her by my side at all these events? Nothing at first, until I learn exactly how risky we might be.

You can order ONCE UPON A WILD FLING everywhere!

ACKNOWLEDGMENTS

I am grateful to many amazing people, including Lauren Clarke, Jen McCoy, Helen Williams, Kim Bias, Virginia, Lynn, Karen, Tiffany, Janice, Stephanie and more for their eyes. Big thanks to Helen for the beautiful cover. Thank you to KP, Kelley, Keyanna and Candi. As always, my readers make everything possible.

ALSO BY LAUREN BLAKELY

FULL PACKAGE, the #1 New York Times Bestselling romantic comedy!

BIG ROCK, the hit New York Times Bestselling standalone romantic comedy!

MISTER O, also a New York Times Bestselling standalone romantic comedy!

WELL HUNG, a New York Times Bestselling standalone romantic comedy!

JOY RIDE, a USA Today Bestselling standalone romantic comedy!

HARD WOOD, a USA Today Bestselling standalone romantic comedy!

THE SEXY ONE, a New York Times Bestselling bestselling standalone romance!

THE HOT ONE, a USA Today Bestselling bestselling standalone romance!

THE KNOCKED UP PLAN, a multi-week USA Today and Amazon Charts Bestselling bestselling standalone romance!

MOST VALUABLE PLAYBOY, a sexy multi-week USA Today Bestselling sports romance, and MOST LIKELY TO SCORE, a sexy football romance!

THE V CARD, a USA Today Bestselling sinfully sexy romantic comedy!

WANDERLUST, a USA Today Bestselling contemporary romance!

COME AS YOU ARE, a Wall Street Journal and multi-week USA Today Bestselling contemporary romance!

PART-TIME LOVER, a multi-week USA Today Bestselling contemporary romance!

The New York Times and USA Today Bestselling Seductive Nights series including *Night After Night*, *After This Night*, and *One More Night*

And the two standalone romance novels in the Joy Delivered Duet, *Nights With Him* and Forbidden Nights, both New York Times and USA Today Bestsellers!

Sweet Sinful Nights, Sinful Desire, Sinful Longing and Sinful Love, the complete New York Times Bestselling high-heat romantic suspense series that spins off from Seductive Nights!

Playing With Her Heart, a USA Today bestseller, and a sexy Seductive Nights spin-off standalone! (Davis and Jill's romance)

21 Stolen Kisses, the USA Today Bestselling forbidden new adult romance!

Caught Up In Us, a New York Times and USA Today Bestseller! (Kat and Bryan's romance!)

Pretending He's Mine, a Barnes & Noble and iBooks Bestseller! (Reeve & Sutton's romance)

Trophy Husband, a New York Times and USA Today Bestseller! (Chris & McKenna's romance)

Far Too Tempting, the USA Today Bestselling standalone romance! (Matthew and Jane's romance)

Stars in Their Eyes, an iBooks bestseller! (William and Jess' romance)

My USA Today bestselling No Regrets series that includes

The Thrill of It (Meet Harley and Trey)

and its sequel

Every Second With You

My New York Times and USA Today Bestselling Fighting Fire series that includes

Burn For Me (Smith and Jamie's romance!)

Melt for Him (Megan and Becker's romance!)

and *Consumed by You* (Travis and Cara's romance!)

The Sapphire Affair series...

The Sapphire Affair

The Sapphire Heist

Out of Bounds

A New York Times Bestselling sexy sports romance

The Only One

A second chance love story!

Stud Finder

A sexy, flirty romance!

CONTACT

I love hearing from readers! You can find me on Twitter at LaurenBlakely3, Instagram at LaurenBlakelyBooks, Facebook at LaurenBlakelyBooks, or online at LaurenBlakely.com. You can also email me at laurenblakelybooks@gmail.com

Printed in Poland
by Amazon Fulfillment
Poland Sp. z o.o., Wrocław

49176242R00172